NORA HILLS, TEXAS | BOOK ONE

# RUMORS OF

*Grace*

## RENA BELL YEAGER

Rumors of Grace

© 2025 by Rena Bell Yeager

All Scripture is quoted from the New International Version.

Note: This novel is a work of fiction. Names, characters, places, and incidents are either products of the author's imagination or used fictitiously. All characters are fictional, and any similarity to people living or dead, is purely coincidental.

Edited by: Kim Richardson, Tri-Epsilon Productions, LLC

Cover by: Emilie Haney, EAHcreative.com

Amazon ISBN - 979 -8-9985066-7-3

Amazon ISBN – ebook - 979-8-9985066-2-8

Ingram ISBN – print - 979-8-9985066-3-5

PIXLEY KNOB PRESS

*To cowboys everywhere.*
*Yee-haw!*

# ONE

GEORGIA STEPPED out of the bookstore on the town square and walked straight to her car, parked in front of the store next door. Head down reading a message on her phone, she stopped when she came to a long black-booted leg, stuck out in front of her. She almost tripped before a voice stopped her, and a hand caught her elbow.

"Hey darlin'. Is that your little car out there? It looks like a smushed stink bug on wheels. It's cute and all, but it wouldn't even hold a bale of hay. And it's blocking my truck."

Georgia looked up from the blue-jeaned leg to the cowboy it was attached to. Tall Black Hat Guy is what most dreamy-eyed girls and a few older women called him. Something between a smirk and a smile graced his rugged face. She was stunned for just a moment, but quickly recovered her voice, and her focus.

"My stink bug, as you called it, is a hybrid. It probably gets five times better mileage than that gas guzzler you're leaning against." She pointed at his truck, then crossed her arms, one eyebrow raised. "And I was only in there five minutes."

He adjusted his black hat on his head, squinting as he did. "My truck is a diesel. And sweetheart, this is Texas. We've got oil on tap." His voice was gritty and caused a small flip in her stomach. Was that a grin on his face or a grimace?

"I've been waiting here at least twenty minutes, darlin." He continued to stare at her, arms crossed at his muscled chest and legs now crossed at his boots.

She squinted back at him, wrinkling her nose as she did. "Well. If you'll excuse me, my hybrid and I will move right now and get out of your hair."

Tall Black Hat Guy stuck his hand out, the grinning smirk now obvious. "Tyler Grant, at your service. I have an idea first." When she didn't shake his hand, he scooted his hat backwards on his head, scratched his forehead, and set it back into place. The old, faded hat looked like it had been stomped on by an angry bull once or twice. She wondered if it was on his head at the time.

"An idea? What could that possibly be, cowboy?" Georgia crossed her arms and frowned, uncertain of his motive. His eyes were smoldering. Smoky gray with something hidden deep in them, like a fire ready to burst into flame. Or was it the Texas heat?

She shook her head. It was hot today. But so was he. The weatherman had said it would be ninety degrees. Hot for an early spring. But the man in front of her was hovering at a hundred. Degrees and percent. She fanned her face, then scratched her neck after realizing what she was doing.

His lips spread into a full-blown lazy smile, and he stuck a hand in one pocket like he knew what she was thinking. Like he knew how she was going to answer his next question. She took a step back.

"How about a date? I figure since I have spent so much time waiting for you and all."

"What?" He couldn't possibly mean what she thought he said. Feeling a blush rise on her face that she knew had nothing to do with the weather, she looked around, sure he wasn't talking to her.

She had heard the rumors about Tyler. How he had broken more than a few hearts. Based on the women she had seen him with before, she wasn't his type, and she knew it. Why in the world would he want a date with her?

She watched the local law enforcement drive past where her car was blocking Tyler's truck, and turned back to him. "Um, I need to move my car before I get a ticket. So can you, um, let me through? Please?"

"Hand me your keys. I'll move it for you." He straightened as he made the offer and stood in front of her, blocking her path as he held out his hand. She shook her head again. Why was he doing this? What was he really after? Surely, he was teasing. She was just a local school teacher, not one of his normal barflies.

"No, thanks. I'll get it." She tried scooting by him again.

He softened his gaze. "Okay. But let me talk to him first." He tipped his thumb back over his shoulder. The local deputy had come around the square again and stopped in front of her car. Tyler waved and trotted over to the officer.

Georgia watched from the sidewalk as Tyler and the officer talked for a bit. He gestured toward her a couple of times and the officer gave her a discerning look. Then the officer nodded at Tyler with a smile, returned to his car and pulled away.

She watched as Tyler sauntered back to the sidewalk with that confident cowboy swagger that her friends all said made them swoon. Then he stood expectantly in front of her again, a triumphant smile spreading wide, having just rescued her from the evil sheriff like a modern-day Robin Hood. What can one date hurt?

"You're asking me out?" The words were out of her mouth before she could stop them.

"One date. At the ranch." He settled his tall, lean body against his truck.

"Why? I mean, why me?"

He leaned closer, his face near to hers. "Why not?"

Her head warred with itself. This was too tempting. Georgia hadn't had a decent date in months. And her last few dates before that had been either less than exciting, or less than gentlemanly. But this was Tyler. And he was not known in the rumor mill for being a gentleman.

"What kind of date?" *And why am I even thinking of doing this?*

The smile spread across his face, like warm butter on bread fresh from the oven.

"Because you're intrigued."

"I'm not. . ."

"Oh, yes you are, sweetheart." He cut her off before she could finish the sentence. "I can see it in those incredible green eyes. So. Whattaya say?"

Tyler Grant was asking for a date. And she, the strait-laced school teacher, the one who everybody knew would someday 'settle down with a nice young man,' was going to say 'Yes.' The town would be shocked. The little old ladies in her church would gossip. Her sister would freak out. Her brother-in-law, well, he would not be happy, at all.

"What should I wear?" It was a safe question. That should give her some idea of his plans, since he hadn't answered her first question. Doubt warred with appeal. Her heart flipped again. Maybe she should check in with a doctor. Or a shrink.

"You look fine the way you are. We'll keep it simple. Maybe a picnic by the lake at the ranch. I'll pick you up Friday at seven. Will that work for you?"

She glanced down at her jeans and blue, simple collared blouse. A row of tiny ruffles bordered the line of buttons up the front. Her auburn hair swung from her everyday ponytail. Very conservative. And not his normal type. She should probably ask for more details, but didn't.

"Um. Okay. I guess one date won't hurt. But I can meet you at the ranch."

"Oh, no. A gentleman always picks up his lady." He tipped his hat and grinned again, turning to walk away.

"Wait. What's your number? I'll send my address to you." She pulled her phone from her hip pocket, where she had stuck it while Tyler talked to the deputy.

"Oh, I know where you live. You're the teacher who lives in the apartments at the end of Ford Street. Between the two little old ladies."

"What? How did you. . ."

Tyler cut her off and nodded his head toward Georgia's vehicle. "You better move your stink bug now. Jim won't let you off twice."

She fisted her keys and hurried to her car. Tyler and the officer were on a first-name basis. Was that good, or bad?

---

GEORGIA DRESSED CASUALLY but carefully for their date. She didn't want to admit that she was attracted to Tyler. She was just doing this out of curiosity more than anything else.

Since he said it was just a picnic, she dressed simply in jeans, a blue flowered blouse, and flat shoes. Looking into the mirror over her bathroom vanity, she brushed her long hair until it gleamed around her shoulders, wondering if she should leave it down. Would it impress him? Was she trying to impress him? She felt a little bit nervous, wondering what he had in mind. After all, this was Tyler. The guy that every female in Nora Hills had a little bit of a crush on. Including herself.

Blowing out a slow breath, she put her hair back into a ponytail. That was definitely more comfortable.

It was just one date. It would likely lead to nothing. Besides, she was not sure she wanted it to lead anywhere. She thought about the string of broken hearts he had left behind, according to the local gossip.

Georgia had not told her sister Ellen she had a date with Tyler. She knew what kind of response she would get. There would be a lecture about Tyler's reputation and going out with a "guy like him." Ellen would likely want to track her on her phone through one of those Find My Family apps. Georgia shuddered. Ellen may be the older sister, but Georgia did not need to be sheltered. She could handle herself just fine.

She had lived by herself, in the apartment between the two older ladies, for the past five years. Before that, she shared an apartment with Ellen, which saved them both money. But then Ellen and Sam got married and bought a house. Although they had offered to let her continue living with them, Georgia didn't want to be a third wheel. Or a spare tire. Or any of the other analogies that could describe the odd man out.

So she found a roommate and moved into the apartment, enjoying her life as a teacher. But in the past few days, since Tyler asked her out, she had started wondering if there was something missing. She was nearly thirty years old, and her roommate had married and moved out two years ago. Maybe she needed to start putting herself out there. Find a nice young man to date, and maybe even marry. Maybe this was a start. She shook her head. That was too many maybes. She would just enjoy herself tonight.

TYLER WALKED into the bunkhouse after spending the day checking for new calves in the upper pasture. Calving season was time-consuming. A cow could drop a calf at any time of the day or night, but it was rewarding to watch the new little lives as they scampered around the fields.

He tossed his hat onto his bed and looked in the mirror. He needed to clean off the grime that covered him. And the stink. He wore the same clothes every day. Wrangler jeans, a button up flannel shirt in the winter or a T-shirt in the summer, and a brown belt with a nondescript buckle. Today, he would dress up just a bit. Scruff shaved clean, light aftershave. Plaid cotton button-up shirt, sleeves rolled up to just below his elbows. His best Wranglers, that weren't new, but not as worn as the others. Black boots with scroll work on the uppers, a belt with the same scrollwork, and a shiny silver buckle. He frowned at his reflection in his small mirror. It would have to do.

Tyler liked living in the bunkhouse, but sometimes it got a little cramped. There was room for eight ranch hands and right now it was completely full. Each had their own room with a full-sized bed rather than a traditional bunk. Mr. Hudson took good care of his crew and made sure they had all the comforts they needed. He didn't want any of his cowboys complaining about beds so short their feet hung over the end.

They were all grown men of varying ages, but most were in their twenties. He was one of the old guys at thirty-three. It didn't make sense to live off-site since the accommodations were included in their pay. Nine years was a long time to live with a bunch of rowdy men, but it suited his needs.

"You're taking out the teacher? Seriously?" Reggie was another ranch hand and Tyler's friend. Tyler watched him in the mirror while combing his dark wavy hair into place. He wondered if Reggie wasn't just a little jealous. Tonight, he felt like he had won the lottery.

He had surprised himself at his own suggestion. Georgia Duncan was an eighth-grade teacher at the local Nora Hills Middle School. Clean cut, oozing sweetness, always wearing a smile and the cutest outfits—never in a ratty T-shirt or torn jeans, even though they were in style.

He hadn't intended to ask her out. Heck, he didn't even know who the car belonged to as he waited. But when he saw her come out of the bookstore, he couldn't stop himself. He had often admired her from afar, knowing she was not the kind of woman he would normally pursue. Even her ponytail reminded him of someone from a movie he had once seen. He almost expected Georgia to break out into song and smiled inwardly at the image that thought provoked.

So now they had a date. This couldn't be one of his typical beer and boot-scootin' nights. Georgia was different. She had probably never touched a drop of alcohol and only danced at weddings. In fact, he recalled that was where he had seen her the first time. At his boss's wedding last year. She had slipped out the door of the reception, leaving before he could catch up to her. But she had captivated him for some reason.

The guys all admired Georgia from afar, and any one of them might have asked her out. But they all liked to get a bit rowdy on the weekends. Tyler and Reggie would normally hit the bars together, and split up at some point when they met their selected girls for the night.

He dusted off his faded black hat before placing it carefully on his head, turning to answer Reggie's question. "Yep. I'm taking out the teacher." Adjusting his hat slightly, he then picked up his keys, tossing them in his hand to make them jingle. His smile grew as he thought about how his date with Georgia would go.

Reggie looked at him like he had gone loco. "Well, if you need backup, don't call me. I'm going into town to find some action. While I'm dancing with a pretty girl, you'll be courtin' the schoolmarm." Reggie laughed at his joke.

Tyler smirked. "No problem, bro. I've got this one covered all by myself."

Yep. An evening by the lake. A picnic, a checkered blanket, and cool sweet tea was definitely called for. The guys might give him a ribbing for it. They would, after all, be out in the open where anyone could see them. But he grinned as he thought about the evening ahead.

As he walked to his truck, one of the hands whistled, a shrill wolf call. He grinned. Let them laugh. They were all just jealous.

# TWO

GEORGIA HEARD the knock at her door and jumped, wondering if she had thought this through before agreeing to the date. She ran her hands over her clothes and hair one more time, making sure she had no wrinkles anywhere. She swallowed hard and opened the door.

Tyler was holding his hand up, ready to knock again. A wide grin spread across his face when their eyes met. She gulped and stepped back a couple of steps. He had been leaning against his truck when they spoke on the square, so she hadn't realized just how tall he was. Or how muscular. There was no doubt he could pick up her five-foot three-inch frame and throw her over his shoulder in one smooth move.

"You ready to go?" His voice sucked her in, pulling her out the door before she knew what she was doing. It wasn't smooth. Sort of gravelly, in a nice way. She swallowed again.

"We're taking your truck?" It was a rhetorical question. Of course, he had driven his truck. When he opened the passenger door for her, she also realized it was taller than she had remembered. How was she going to climb into this behemoth? It had four rear tires instead of two, extra-large exhaust pipes, and breathed diesel fuel. And what was that hanging off the hitch? The metal replica of bull anatomy swung gingerly and she quickly averted her eyes, focusing on the front of the truck. The custom cattle pusher, mounted over the grill, looked like it was specially built to move an elephant.

Georgia watched as Tyler opened the door behind her seat and pulled out a stool. How embarrassing. She knew he was probably just trying to be nice and was impressed he had anticipated the need for the stool, but she wondered what her neighbors were thinking right now. She had seen the curtains pulled back slightly from the windows in the apartments on each side of her. The two ladies were friendly enough, but they were certainly nosy.

Tyler steadied her as she climbed into the cab. His hands on her waist were warm, and left a little sizzle when he removed them to shut her door. Inhaling deeply, his cologne invaded her nose, mingling with the scent of horse, hay, and leather that permeated the truck. Settling into her seat, she smoothed her hands down her jeans again to compose her nerves. She hoped he would be as courteous all night. He rapped his knuckles on the hood of his truck as he rounded the front, looking pleased with himself, and easily slipped behind the steering wheel.

⸱⸱————⸱⸱

THE DOUBLE H Ranch sat fifteen miles outside of the town limits and was one of the largest ranches in the area. Nora Hills was a small town on the North Fork of the Guadalupe River, on the western edge of Texas Hill Country. Rolling hills eventually gave way to flat terrain toward the west. Pecan groves dotted the landscape up and down the river. Bald cypress trees were also plentiful in the area. Most ranchers raised beef cattle and longhorns. Some raised horses. Area farms grew a variety of grains and beans, in addition to alfalfa and other grasses for hay. Small farm markets were often set up along roadsides, selling their locally grown vegetables.

She watched out the window as the miles slipped by before finally turning her attention to Tyler, studying his profile. His eyes were on the road, but he had a silly grin on his face, as if he had received the grand prize ribbon at the county fair for his mama's homemade pickles. His face was sturdy if a bit ruddy, having spent years in the saddle under the hot Texas sun.

The hands gripping the steering wheel were not as weathered but still strong and callused. She could imagine him in worn leather work gloves, fixing a crooked fence post or tagging a new calf. And the view as he bent over to do those things? His jeans did fit him well. She cleared her throat and looked away.

"What were you thinking, darlin'?"

The Texas twang in his words fit him to a $T$, and when she turned toward him, she spied his grin growing even wider. She was busted.

"Just wondering what you had planned. Are we there yet?" She laughed awkwardly at the age-old question.

"Two more miles. It's up ahead on the right."

Everyone knew the Double H Ranch. It was twenty-five thousand acres of the best real estate in the area. They passed by the front gates that hung from the wrought iron archway and drove on to a second gate about a half-mile down the road. This gate was more utilitarian, with simple metal poles holding a single pole overhead. The gates themselves were kind of like stock gates on steroids. They rolled to either side after Tyler punched a code into the security keypad.

"This is the service entrance. One of several, actually. We

have gates on each side of the ranch." Tyler explained the system as they drove up to one side of the lake. The family ranch house stood on a hill overlooking the lake. It was walking distance, but still far enough away for privacy.

"Oh, my. This is beautiful!" Georgia drew in a breath as they rounded the bend in the long driveway and the lake came into view. It was eighty acres of pristine beauty that had been built by the Hudson family to supply water to the self-sustaining ranch. She was amazed at the sparkling water and perfectly mowed shoreline. Trees dotted the shore as well, and she could see a boathouse in the distance with an attached dock. The Double H was a resort, as well as a working ranch.

Tyler parked the truck in a gravel lot near the lake. He went around to the passenger door, ready to help Georgia down but she hopped out the door. Getting out of the truck was much easier than getting in.

"You beat me to it. I was hoping to show you how refined I can be." His grin was wide, gray eyes twinkling. He gathered the blanket and cooler from the back seat and walked with Georgia to the spot he had chosen for the picnic. A large red barn stood nearby.

They walked up the hill, finding shade under a live oak tree. It was a good spot to spread the blanket that Tyler had tucked into the picnic basket along with the food. The view from the spot was stunning as the water shimmered in the evening sun.

"This picnic was a great idea. And this chicken salad on a croissant is better than any I have tasted anywhere. Did you make it?" Georgia held the sandwich that Tyler had brought for her, savoring its delicious flavor. The buttery flakiness practically melted in her mouth. It was definitely not purchased at the local deli. She turned to Tyler and noticed he had nearly devoured his sandwich. She teased him with her question.

Tyler laughed. "I got them from the cook at the guest house. That's at the resort, on the other side of the ranch. This is the family side. The cook there takes care of me." His wide smile seemed to be pasted on. "Anyway, they had it for lunch today. But my favorite is the chips. Homemade. Crunchy and yummy." He emphasized his point by popping a chip into his mouth with a loud munch.

They sat in silence for several minutes, finishing their meal before Georgia spoke again.

"It is so peaceful out here." She admired the quiet of the lake and turned to see Tyler watching her.

"Yeah, I think that is what has drawn me to this place. Why I've stayed here for nine years." Tyler adjusted his hat.

"Nine years? That's a long time. I've only been teaching for six years."

"It's a long story." Tyler shrugged and looked away.

Georgia waited for him to say more, but apparently, he wasn't going to.

"Can we go for a walk? I'd like to see more of this beautiful place." Georgia picked up the empty containers and wrappers from the meal and placed them in the cooler. It was a matter of habit to always pick up after herself, but it also helped to hide her nerves. She picked up her bottled water and took a large swallow.

"Sure thing." Tyler rose to his feet, reaching for Georgia's hand as he did. His grip was firm, and she didn't pull away when he wrapped his warm callused fingers around hers.

"Tell me about the ranch. What am I seeing as I look across the lake?"

"Let me show you something first." Tyler led Georgia around the edge of the lake to a spot not far away that she hadn't even noticed. A finger of water stretched between some trees, creating a small private pool. Stepping behind her, he turned her toward the water.

"From here, you can see the family home." He wrapped one arm over her shoulder, not quite touching, but close enough she could smell the scent of his soap. Pointing another direction, he gently guided her hip with his other hand.

"Behind us, which you can't see, is the resort side of the ranch. But over there," he pointed to their left. "See that grove of trees? That's our pecan grove. We sell them in the resort gift shop."

"I love pecans." She leaned her head back to speak. As she did, he leaned his head forward. The foot difference in height was a little awkward.

"We harvest them in the late fall. You'll have to come back then." His voice was like a purr in her ear.

"What about the rest of the ranch? I know there are thousands of acres."

"Twenty-five thousand. The acreage is behind the pecan grove and family home. The bunkhouse, where all the ranch hands live, is behind the barn. Our stables are over on the right, behind the first barn on the hill."

"It's beautiful here. I can't believe you get to see this every day."

Tyler laughed in her ear and took her hand again. "Not exactly. Most of the time, I only get to see dusty bovines and fallen fence wire." He led her out of the trees back to the lake and shifted his hand in hers, linking them together.

"Can I ask you a question?" She swiveled to face him.

"That sounds serious." He lifted an eyebrow.

"Not really. But this is all about getting to know each other. Right?"

He nodded slowly, his face uncertain as he faced her.

"Tell me. Who is Tyler Grant? I mean, I've heard the word

on the street, but you don't seem like that kind of guy to me."
She watched as he considered her question, his eyes turned
upward toward the sky before looking back at her.

"I can imagine what you've heard. But I'm just a cowboy.
Nobody special." He pushed his hat back and scratched his
forehead with his free hand before setting it again on his head.
His voice was like a dust devil. All sand and air that left her
heart in a whirlwind. But there was pain in his answer.

"We're all special in some way, Tyler." She stopped and
twisted to look at him fully.

A breeze caught her ponytail and whipped it in front of her
face. He lifted a finger to swipe it away from her mouth, and
she took his hand in hers.

"Look at your hands, Tyler."

He squinted his eyes. "Why?"

Georgia then took both of his hands and turned them palms
up, running her thumbs over his calluses. She noticed his
empty ring finger. There has never been a ring there, according
to town gossip, and she briefly wondered why. She took a
breath to pull her thoughts back in and turned her face up in a
smile.

"You are obviously not afraid of hard work. I bet you have
pulled and replaced a lot of fence posts. Ridden all day in the
sun, wrangling calves, or whatever you call it. That shows
strength and perseverance to me."

She traced the lines on one hand before closing his fingers,
but held open his thumb. "And look at your thumb. See that?
That's your thumbprint. Nobody else in the world has your
thumbprint." She wrapped her fingers around his thumb,
holding it up and tracing the lines there. "That makes you
special in the eyes of God. Uniquely you. Maybe the problem is
that people don't know you."

Tyler's eyes grew darker, his gaze over her shoulder to a

place somewhere far away, a frown starting to grow. Georgia watched as emotions flitted across his face. But then he turned the corners of his lips up. He flipped her hands palm up, his thumbs caressing her palms.

"Look at your hands, Georgia. Soft, smooth, and graceful. Who are you?"

An eyebrow arched over his smokey eyes. She searched his face for a moment before her lips spread in a slow smile, a slight shrug of her shoulders. "I'm just a teacher. Nobody special."

"*Au contraire.* You touch the lives of kids every day. And in teaching them that they are special, it makes you special." She smiled as he linked their fingers together.

They continued their walk again, hand in hand, and soon returned to the blanket.

"What is it like to be a cowboy? I mean, I really don't know much about a working ranch." She picked up a leaf that had fallen in front of her and twirled it in her fingers.

Tyler leaned back on one elbow, his eyes absorbing hers as she twirled the leaf in her hand. Several leaves rained around them as the live oak went through its annual spring leaf drop.

"You were right when you said I spend most of my day in the sun. The cattle eat the grass pretty close to the ground, so we have to move them from time to time and give the grass time to grow. I spend most of my time in the saddle, nudging them around. Cap is my horse, and as far as animals go, one of my best friends." He paused.

"Don't most ranches use ATVs today? I thought being a cowboy was kind of a lost art."

Tyler chuckled. "We have eight ranch hands here, in addition to the boss and his son. We are all cowboys. And although we use ATVs for some things, we prefer horses. There is less noise, less pollution, and we can go places that a vehicle can't easily go."

Georgia tossed the leaf aside and adjusted her legs to get more comfortable. "I don't know how to ride. I'm not sure I have the strength to hang on. That, and my body and brain aren't always coordinated. I would probably fall off."

"You can learn to ride, and I can teach you sometime if you want. Me, I've got glue on my butt, or so I've been told. It just seems to come naturally for me."

The thought of riding with Tyler put a new image in her mind. To ride together held great appeal, with her in front and him closely behind her, arms around her as he held the reins. A scene straight out of an old Western movie.

Tyler relaxed on the blanket with his hands behind his head. "Sure is turning into a pretty sunset. This is one of my favorite spots on the ranch." He lifted his arm to point at the lake, where a family of ducks swam lazily across the water.

Georgia laid back against the tree, her eyes on the beauty in front of them. He scooted her closer, then propped up on his elbow to gaze at her. They stared at each other for a moment.

"You've got a leaf in your hair." He said it so quietly, it was almost a whisper. He picked the leaf out of her ponytail, and feathered it down her jawline. She leaned into the movement, closing her eyes, and opening them again as she heard his shift.

He tossed the leaf aside and leaned closer, his eyes focused on hers. He looked so. . . intense.

"What would you say if I kissed you?" He ran his finger along the same jawline he had just caressed with the leaf. She hadn't expected this question. She thought she might get a kiss at her door, when he took her home. But then he spoke again in her ear, his words so light she almost didn't understand him at first.

"Wanna go hide in the barn?"

"Do I want to what?" She slammed her hand into his rock-hard chest and scrambled to her feet. His grunt was just what she would have expected. *Caveman!* Yes, she had heard the rumors. She knew his reputation. But she had not heeded the warnings.

"No! I do not want to go hide in the barn. What makes you think I would want to do that?"

"Georgia. . ." He tilted his hat and scratched his head as he sat up.

"You think every girl is going to swoon at your feet because you're handsome? Well, guess again! I am not one of your conquests!" Georgia stomped away from him, not caring where she was going.

"Hey! You're going the wrong way,"

Georgia stopped and turned. What did he just say?

"The truck is that way, in the parking lot. You're headed toward the house." Georgia followed Tyler's arm with her eyes as he pointed in the opposite direction.

Tears stood on the edge of her eyelids. "I just want to go home." It was then she realized she didn't have her car. Big mistake.

"Look. I'm sorry. Let's go to the truck." His voice was softer and he seemed sincere, but Georgia had had enough.

"No, I'll call Ellen." She pulled out her phone and dialed her sister, but there was no answer. Grumbling, she placed her phone back into her pocket, then put her hands on her hips and looked around, wondering what to do next. Why hadn't she insisted on driving her car and meeting him here? Now she was stuck. Her brain pointed an accusing finger back at her. *Let that be a lesson to you, Georgia Duncan.*

She spied Mrs. Hudson sitting in a glider on the porch of the large ranch house and stomped in her direction.

"Are you okay, dear?" Georgia saw sympathy in Rachel Hudson's eyes. Maybe she could help.

"I'm okay. I just feel like an idiot." She smacked her forehead with one hand.

Rachel chuckled. "Men are the idiots, dear. We just fall for them."

Tyler cleared his throat from behind her. "I'm sorry, Georgia. Really. Let me take you home." He was just a couple of feet away, slapping his hat against his leg, a wave of hair over his forehead. He actually sounded contrite.

Georgia looked at Rachel, pleading with her eyes.

"Tyler?" Rachel's eyes wavered between the two of them.

"I'll take her. If she wants me to."

"Georgia? Do you want Tyler to take you home?" When Georgia shook her head, Rachel turned to Tyler.

"That's okay, Tyler. Matthew is in the house. He can take her home and pick up some of Annie's favorite ice cream while he is in town. That girl and her cravings. I wanted the same things when I was pregnant with her." Rachel shook her head.

Georgia knew that Matthew was Mr. Hudson's son, and that he ran most of the ranch. She hated to inconvenience him, but she didn't see any other way out. Her date with Tyler was officially over.

# THREE

MONDAY MORNING, Tyler and Reggie rode together toward one of the remote pastures, looking for stray cows. It gave him time to think about his date with Georgia. What went right, and what went wrong.

He had noticed that she listened intently when he spoke about his ranch life, taking in everything he said as if she was genuinely interested. She was perky, and well-respected in their small town. He wondered about her story, and what she would think if she knew his.

Although he knew he had insulted her, he enjoyed watching her walk away, fire in her eyes and a sway to her blue-jeaned hips. He had known who she was for quite some time, but had never thought much about her until she blocked his truck with her car. He wasn't really in a hurry that day, but it gave him the opportunity to tease a pretty girl. And he loved to tease pretty girls.

Maybe she was right. Maybe he did deserve her angry response. But he wasn't really the cad Georgia seemed to think he was. He didn't do one-night stands. When he took a girl out, they had fun. And maybe a little necking. Then he took her home. But somewhere along the way, someone had implied much more, and the stories had grown like the proverbial fish that got away.

That he had ignored the gossip was something he hadn't thought about before. But Georgia's reaction whispered to him that it might be time to start looking for a serious relationship. Settle down. Create some stability in his life. But the gossip might get in his way.

Reggie looked sideways at Tyler as they rode together to move cattle to a new pasture. "What's the smile about? I thought the date was a bust."

"It wasn't that bad. I just rushed her. Maybe she'll go out with me again."

Tyler really did want a second date. He would take her somewhere they could spend time together without the worry of physical expectations and just have fun. It surprised him to even think that way. There was something about her that made him think wholesome thoughts, and it scared him just a little. Reggie's response burst his bubble.

"You're dreaming, Tyler. Georgia is out of your league and mine. She is too sweet. Sugary sweet." Reggie shuddered. "You and I are more like rough-cut lumber. Georgia is fine trim work, smooth and silky, decorating the finest drawing rooms. We are bunkhouse all the way." He waved his hand as he spoke, like a game show host.

Tyler had told Reggie some of his background, but he hadn't admitted that there was actually a little bit of drawing room in his family tree. Tyler had walked away from that nine years ago. Was Georgia pulling him back in?

"I don't know what to do, Reg. I want to see her again. On the other hand, she may tell me to buzz off." He swatted at a fly that was buzzing his head.

"Man, you have never been at a loss for words. So she shot you down. Try again." Reggie shot him a glance. "For a guy who can pick up any girl in any bar, this should be a piece of cake." He paused again. "Tell you what. . . send her a text. Tell her how beautiful her eyes are and that you want to see them again." Reggie wiggled his eyebrows.

"How do you know how beautiful her eyes are? You been checking her out?" Reggie's comment irked Tyler just a bit.

"We've all seen her around town. We know she's pretty. So whatcha gonna do about it?"

"I can't send her a text." Tyler mumbled.

"Why not?"

"I don't have her number."

Reggie laughed. It was a full on, gut-buster laugh, making his horse look back at him with that *"You okay?"* look.

"How did you ask her out, if you don't have her number?"

"I saw her in town. It was a spur-of-the-moment thing, you know. Her little car was blocking my truck, so I asked her for a date. I was shocked when she actually agreed. And, we all know where she lives, so I didn't need her number." He steered Cap toward a stray heifer, hoping to steer away from the conversation.

"You're slippin', man. You must have it bad for her."

"Shut up." Tyler waved his hat at the cow to redirect her. He was done with this conversation.

"Atta' boy! Go git'er!" Reggie laughed again and rode away after an errant calf as Tyler scowled.

●——————●●

ELLEN BORED her eyes into Georgia, her best parental look.

25

"Why didn't you tell me you were going out with Tyler? I could have told you what would happen."

Telling Ellen the story of the date had stirred Georgia's anger all over again. He had made the inappropriate suggestion, not Georgia. Still, as she thought through everything again, she realized she might have set herself up.

She touched her lips with her fingers. He hadn't even kissed her, but he had been so close, his breath tickling her ear, and she had been very tempted. She shook her head to erase the memory.

"I'm sure this is the end of it, anyway. There is no way he will ever ask me out again, so you don't have to worry about me." Georgia picked up Ellen and Sam's new baby and cuddled him close, enjoying the fresh baby smell. Life is so uncomplicated when you haven't had any experiences yet, like little Sam Junior. Why did it have to be so hard as an adult?

Placing the baby back into his crib, Georgia gave Ellen a hug before turning toward the door, not wanting to return to her lonely apartment. Tyler fascinated her. But she had to accept the inevitable. He was not for her, and she was not for him.

"What would you do if he called you again?" Ellen called out as she wrapped a blanket around her son. "Would you go out with him?"

Georgia watched Ellen tuck little Sam in and wondered, what would a child of Tyler's look like? Would he have those smokey gray eyes like his father? Would he be a magnet to young girls as he grew older?

Why was she thinking like that, anyway?

"You haven't answered me." Some days, Ellen acted more like a mother than a sister.

"He can't call me. He doesn't have my phone number. So it's a moot point."

# FOUR

THE FOLLOWING WEEK, Tyler walked into the Farm and Ranch Store and almost bumped into Sam as he was coming out. Sam would have Georgia's number. Would he give it to him?

"Hey, Sam. Wait up!" Tyler spun on his boot heel and jogged to catch up with him.

Sam kept walking, ignoring Tyler. Tyler followed until they reached Sam's truck.

"Stay away from her." Sam grabbed his door handle and opened the door. Georgia must have told them about the date.

"Whoa." Tyler held up his hands. "I just want to apologize. Nothing happened, I swear it. I just may have said something to her that she didn't take kindly to."

"Yeah, I heard all about your suggestion."

"Well..." He took a deep breath, admitting his *faux pas*. "I'd like to make it right. And I kind of need her phone number to do that."

"She didn't give you her phone number? And you are asking me for it? Why should I give it to you if she didn't?" Sam furrowed his forehead. He stared at Tyler for a full eight seconds. Tyler felt like he was riding a bull, but stood his ground, refusing to blink.

"Look. This is against my better judgement, and she will probably kill me for it," Sam finally said. "Give me your number and I'll pass it on to her. If she wants to talk to you, she'll let you know. And if you hurt her, I'm coming after you."

"Thanks, man." He wasn't sure where this thing was going, and he had no intention of hurting Georgia, but he wasn't giving up without a fight, either. And although he didn't know why, he wouldn't allow himself to examine that question.

SATURDAY MORNING, Tyler drove around the town square. He hadn't heard from Georgia since giving Sam his phone number. He didn't know if that meant Georgia didn't want anything more to do with him, or if Sam had made his own decision to not pass Tyler's number along.

The square was one of the older parts of town, with a three-story Spanish-style courthouse in the center. Most of the buildings still had the Old West feel, with false fronts at the roofline, and adobe facades. A statue of the founding couple stood on the lawn in front of the courthouse. Nora Hills was named after Nora and Frank McCoy, who were the first settlers, having arrived nearly two hundred years earlier. It was originally named by Frank as Nora's Hill, but the name was later changed to make it easier to say. The life-sized bronze sculpture depicted the couple. Him on foot, and her riding her magnificent horse.

The square was busy today. Banks sat on two opposing corners, with restaurants on the other corners. There were two law offices, a clothing store, a personal finance company, and an antique store filling in the spaces. A small drugstore offered a true soda fountain, which only served authentic Blue Bell Ice Cream, in true Texas style. And, tucked away on one side was the bookstore, and next to it, a pastry and coffee shop.

In its early days, there would have been horses and wagons hitched around the square, or down side streets. Today, it was mostly pickup trucks. But while the mode of transportation may have changed, it was still the place to meet and visit on a Saturday morning.

Tyler drove past the bookstore where he had first seen Georgia, and stopped when he saw her car parked there. He blocked her just enough with his truck that she wouldn't be able to leave until he did. He just wanted to talk to her.

When she stepped out of the bookstore, he strode up quickly. She looked good in that small-town girl sort of way. Jeans, a pink sweater, and flat shoes all hugged her nicely without giving too much away. Her ponytail swung around her face as she turned toward her car, a hint of red highlights shining through the brown.

"Hey, Georgia. Got a minute?"

Georgia lifted her head, a startled look on her face, before turning into a frown. "I might have a minute."

"Have coffee with me. My treat." Tyler nodded his head toward the shop next door, walking close enough to touch her, although he didn't.

"I'm not sure that is a good idea." She kept walking toward her car.

Tyler lowered his head and his voice, his hands raised palms up as he begged. "It's a public place, Georgia. I just want to talk. Give me thirty minutes."

Georgia lifted the bag that was in her hand. It looked heavy, and he reached out to take it from her, but she pulled it away from him.

"Okay. I'll give you thirty minutes, and not a minute more. But you'd better move your truck before you get a ticket." Jim, the local deputy, was driving by, and he had his eyes on Tyler's truck. "I'll just stick this in my car," indicating the bag containing the book. "And your time starts now."

Tyler looked at his watch and trotted quickly to his truck to find a new spot. He wasn't sure what he was hoping for out of this conversation, but he hadn't been able to shake her from his mind. And he had a hunch that maybe she would be in the bookstore today, and his smile spread across his face.

Walking back to the coffee shop after parking his truck, he saw another woman walking up the sidewalk toward him. The blonde bombshell was dressed provocatively for a Saturday morning and might have starred as the sexy babe in a music video somewhere.

"Hey, Tyler." She pursed those lips in a mock kiss and swayed by him, not stopping.

Tyler turned on his heels, walking backwards for a few steps to enjoy the rear view. He stopped at the door of the coffee shop, peeling his eyes away to refocus on his goal.

Entering the shop, he noticed the long line. When he walked up to the table by the window where Georgia was already seated, she tapped her watch. "Clock's ticking, cowboy."

There were six people in front of him. "I thought the time would start after we got our coffee."

"I might make an exception. I'll have a cinnamon swirl mocha latte with whipped cream and a maple walnut muffin. I hope you can remember all of that." She smiled at him with the slightest of smirks, tipping only one side of her mouth up. Tyler thought about how long it would take to prepare the order. She wasn't going to make this easy on him. Her message was clear. *"Get it right, cowboy."*

Fortunately, the line proceeded forward quickly and within minutes he had brought their order to the table. He set the tray between them and sat down, soaking in her lovely face.

Georgia looked warily at him as she blew on her coffee to cool it before taking a sip. The whipped cream fluttered with her breath. "You wanted to talk to me?"

He took a sip of his own black coffee, ignoring the muffin he had ordered just because she had ordered one. "Yeah, I wanted to apologize. For, you know, that day by the lake."

"Apology accepted. Thanks for the coffee." She started to gather her purse, coffee, and muffin to leave.

Tyler quickly reached out to intercept her arm. Their eyes locked and he spoke softly to diffuse her irritation. "Come on, Georgia. You said I had thirty minutes."

She looked around, as several people glanced quickly away. Tyler knew they had an audience. He even saw a couple of cell phones pointed in their direction. Georgia sighed and sat back in her chair, waiting for him to continue.

"I was thinking about something a little more tangible." Tyler gave her a pleading look.

Nodding toward the window, Georgia gave him her best "teacher" stare. The one that said she didn't believe him. "You expect me to think you're sincere after that little display outside a few minutes ago?"

"What display?" He hadn't realized she could see him from inside the shop.

"What's her name?" She pulled her hand away from his to cross her arms. Her posture told him she would be a tough sell.

"Um," Tyler couldn't remember, so he made something up. "Darla."

"Last name?" Georgia quirked an eyebrow at him.

31

"I don't remember." She had caught him, and he knew it. Might as well be honest.

"Well, she apparently knew you." Georgia took another sip of her fancy coffee as Tyler squirmed.

"Send daisies." Her head was tilted in challenge.

"Daisies? I don't understand." He was confused, and squinted his eyes together.

"You said something tangible." She shrugged one shoulder. "I like daisies."

"Oh. I was thinking of something else." They weren't getting very far with this conversation. Maybe he wasn't making himself clear.

Georgia sighed, closing her eyes before looking at him again. "What do you want, Tyler?"

Swallowing the coffee he had just sipped, he realized that her frustration had probably reached its limit. "Go out with me again." He held up his hand before she could interrupt. "There is a fair this weekend over at the county seat. We could, you know, just hang out, see the exhibits, ride the rides, eat fried food. Stuff like that. My way of saying I'm sorry." He stuffed a piece of his muffin in his mouth and waited for her answer.

Georgia sat the cup down and tilted her head, one hand on her chin, the other tapping on the table. He watched as she considered his offer before answering. Her thumb and fingers framed her sweet pink lips.

"I'm not sure why I am doing this. But Sam is competing in the rodeo there on Saturday. Maybe we could go then. Against my better judgment, of course. I will expect you to be on your best behavior." She raised one eyebrow. He could imagine her with glasses on her nose, looking over them with that glare.

"Yes, ma'am. And there is a concert after the rodeo. Amos Carver is playing and they are really great. We can stay for that, too. If it's okay with you, that is."

Georgia tapped her smartwatch to check the time. "Okay. I'll go with you to the fair. Bring the daisies."

Tyler grinned in celebration. She was giving him a second chance. He reached across the table for her hand, noticing she had drunk most of her coffee. He needed a way to extend this time with her. "What do you say we take a walk around the square?"

"Why?"

He shrugged. "Just because. I have no ulterior motive, I promise." He grinned at her. "Other than just spending time with a pretty girl." He saw her frown and rubbed her hand with his thumb. "With you, I mean."

He was losing ground. He leaned across the table, taking her hand fully in his. "You're gonna make me work for this, aren't you? Come on. I just wanna see you smile."

"I suppose a walk around the square is okay." She turned up the corners of her mouth. It was a half-smile, but it was better than the frown. "We won't run into any other women whose names you can't remember, will we?"

"Well, I can't guarantee that. The only name I can remember right now is Georgia Duncan."

# FIVE

SEVEN DAYS LATER, Georgia and Tyler were floating over the midway on the double Ferris wheel, topping the apex of its wide arc from top to bottom. He had, indeed, sent flowers from the local florist. The bouquet of daisies and zinnias was still sitting in the middle of her dining room table. And their walk around the square had taken a full hour as they browsed the antique shop and finished at the soda fountain.

"I can't believe you talked me into coming to the fair with you." She had finally given him her phone number. Maybe it was foolish, but she had seen something in him on that first date. And he had been so considerate as they strolled the square last Saturday. She remembered how funny he was as they made up stories about each of the stores on the square, and what it would have been like a hundred years ago. Who knew he had such a creative imagination? She found herself actually looking forward to enjoying the fair with him.

"I thought it would be fun. We'll ride a few rides, wander through the exhibits, and sample a few tasty fried treats. Then we'll watch Sam win the calf roping contest and take in the concert afterwards."

"You're putting a lot of faith in Sam and his roping partner. It takes two to win the team roping event."

"I saw them rope together last year. They were amazing. I have every confidence they will win." Tyler swung the car, rocking it beyond her comfort zone.

"Tyler. Please stop." She grabbed his thigh, squeezing to hold herself steady.

"Yes, ma'am. I guess you don't like this? I'll keep you safe." He wrapped his arm around her shoulders.

"I get motion sickness. But usually I can handle the Ferris wheel."

"Never fear. We will sit completely still, just like this, until the end of the ride." He squeezed her shoulder and gave her a crooked smile.

*Goofball.* He knew exactly what he was doing.

The weather was typical of Texas Hill Country in late March. Not too hot, but warm enough they only needed a light jacket. They wandered around the midway for a while, trying out the treats and playing a few of the games. Tyler showed off his muscles when he rang the bell with the sledgehammer. They walked through the fun house, making fun of themselves as they first looked round, and then skinny in the distorted mirrors.

"Let's go see the animals." Georgia allowed him to grab her hand, pulling her toward the barns. She was amazed at how clean the stalls were. Tyler explained that was part of how they were judged, in addition to judging the animals themselves. Even the pigs were clean. She loved watching the little squealers as they raced around a track, an Oreo cookie as the prize for the fastest pig.

"I'd race for an Oreo!" Tyler rubbed his rock-hard stomach and chuckled.

"Poor baby. I'll buy you a package of Oreos if you are that hard up." Georgia patted his abs. Yep. They were like concrete. He grabbed her hand and held it there, his eyes on hers.

"I'll take you up on that." His gaze was intense, and Georgia pulled her eyes away first.

They wandered through the cattle barn. Georgia stared in awe at a Brahma bull that a young boy was leading around a small indoor arena. The two-thousand-pound bull had intelligent eyes, and was compliant in the smaller boy's hands. The crowd of mostly exhibitors remained silent so as not to disturb the pair, then let out a collective sigh and applause as they won the purple ribbon. Georgia sighed as well, not realizing she had been holding her breath. Tyler squeezed her hand and her cheeks turned pink. She started to get a new appreciation for him, and for what the cowboys do every day.

"How large are the cattle you work with? Are you ever in danger?" Watching the display had made Georgia wonder just how hard the life of a cowboy might be.

"Big. Very big." Tyler held his arms out wide. "The cows are large enough, but bulls can range between a thousand and two thousand pounds. And a ton of angry bull is nothing to mess with. You can get stomped on or thrown into a fence if you aren't paying attention. That usually happens when you are trying to move a bull from a pen or stock trailer. I've been jostled around a time or two—gotten stepped on once or twice. But for the most part, our cattle are pretty docile. And the Brahma bulls are normally calm. That little boy in there was never in any danger."

Georgia thought about what he had just said. Most of what she knew came from books. Tyler's knowledge came from experience. Her appreciation grew another notch.

Leaving the barn, she pulled Tyler into another building next door, where there was an exhibit of butterflies that was provided by a local ranch. "Did you know that Monarch butterflies migrate from Canada to Mexico every fall, and their path goes right over Nora Hills? They can even track the swarms on radar. This ranch tags and monitors some of the butterflies." This exhibit consisted of monarchs and snout-nosed moths.

"How do you know all of this?" His eyes gleamed like glass.

"We did a study of the butterflies in class." She grinned like a Cheshire Cat.

"Of course you did." He shook his head. "And what about the moths? I can understand tracking the butterflies. But a moth?"

Georgia's eyes lit up as she explained the moth. Teaching was her gig. "This moth is a cousin to the monarch so they are often found together. It's not as exquisite as the butterfly, but some of the moths can be quite handsome. They are known as the bug most likely to end up on your windshield at night because they are attracted to the headlights."

•—————•

TYLER WONDERED what Georgia was thinking as she explained about the insects. He imagined she was a good teacher, exciting her students about whatever subject she was sharing with them. She was definitely a monarch. Beautiful and graceful, a royal princess. But he felt more like the moth. He had hit hard several times in his life, his face flat against the windshield. She was like a beacon and he was really attracted to her. He just hoped he didn't end up against the glass.

She tugged on his hand while his mind wandered, and before he knew it, they were in front of an exhibit of quilts.

Georgia oohed and awed over the intricate designs. Tyler groaned. Quilts were fine as long as they kept you warm. Otherwise, they were just another piece of cloth. He didn't really care much about the exhibit, but he loved guiding her with his hand on her back as they wandered through the display. Her eyes lit up at the myriad of patterns and colors. To him, it was simply a warm blanket for a cold night.

Georgia's smile brightened as she admired an exquisite quilt of multi-colored circles, running her hand softly over the soft cotton. It had an intricate pattern of stitching inside the circles. "Ooh. I love this pattern. This is called a double wedding ring. Each tiny piece is sewn by hand, and some have thousands of tiny pieces. They were traditionally made by the church or community for a new bride as a wedding present. It's a true gift of love." Georgia beamed as she shared the information, but talk of weddings made Tyler uncomfortable.

"That's interesting. But enough of this. We came here to cut loose and have fun. Let's go ride that scrambling ride." Tyler grabbed her hand and wiggled his eyebrows at Georgia, turning her away from the quilts. He needed to change the pace and add something wild. "Oh, wait. You said you get motion sickness." He felt chagrined at the look of horror on her face.

"I do, yes. But if I keep my eyes closed, maybe it won't be too bad. However—and I'm telling you—if I throw up and it splatters everywhere—don't say I didn't warn you."

"Would you really throw up?" Maybe he should rethink this.

"I think I will be okay for one ride. But just one. Besides, it might be fun to smush you against the side of the car."

Typical. The girls always wanted to be the *smusher*. "So you're game?"

Georgia tilted her head and turned up her mouth in a sly grin. "Might be payback, if you know what I mean."

Tyler adjusted his hat and pulled her outside into the bright sun. He guided her back to the midway where they found the ride, and he bought their tickets. When it was their turn to board, he held her waist and helped her into the seat before climbing in behind her. He slid into the outside corner so he was facing her, then wrapped his arm around her shoulders, pulling her back against him.

"Might as well get cozy now." Georgia elbowed his stomach, but settled in, and Tyler put his arm around her on the back of the seat. The attendant gave the seat a push which made it start rocking and she slid further into him.

"You okay?" Tyler's gravelly voice tickled her ear.

"I'm good. But thanks for asking." He was looking forward to holding her so closely. Despite their earlier date, this one had been fun, so far.

They were the last couple to load. The ride started slow, moving in circles in and out as it spun in a larger circle on the outside. The attendant bumped up the speed, throwing Georgia hard against Tyler's chest. He reached up to grab his hat to keep it from flying off, and wrapped his arm more firmly around her, hat in hand. His pulse raced, and he wondered if she felt the same way.

The ride spun even faster again and threw her head back against his jaw with a clunk. It was a dizzying experience, but not just from the ride. They laughed together, and he held her tighter as the operator increased the speed yet again. She was practically on top of him now, and he was loving it. These rides were usually pretty short. But there had not been many people in line, so the operator appeared to be giving them extra time. Round, and round, and round, they twirled until all the colors and sounds of the fair blended into an abstract haze.

All too soon, the ride was over. She shook her head while it slowed to a stop and her ponytail smacked him in the face. He tugged on it in jest before settling his hat on his head.

"Wow. I had forgotten how crazy that ride could be." Georgia laughed as Tyler lifted her from the seat, throwing his arm around her shoulder again as she stumbled.

"I think I'm a bit woozy. You may have to hold me up until my head stops spinning."

He tightened his arm to draw her closer. "Let's go get something to drink. I am dying of thirst now, anyway." Tyler grinned. He had no idea that simply spending time together could be so much fun. He steered her to a gray cloud that rose from the smoker where the brisket had been cooking all day. Tyler ordered two sandwiches and big lemon drinks. Georgia added lettuce and mayonnaise to her sandwich, and he took note of her conservative preference. He liked his sandwiches spicy, and added mustard, jalapenos, and pickles.

They sat down at one of the picnic tables nearby, taking in the sights and sounds of the fair. Kids ran everywhere, and parents tried to keep up. Lights flashed from the rides and the food stands, music blared as a ride took off in a crazy, spinning loop. One stand advertised they would fry anything. Elephant ears, pickles, ice cream, or even donuts. Why would you fry a donut again? They laughed together as they watched the crowd, moaning over the calorie-filled treats. He watched her as they ate, and thought for the first time he might be falling in love. But this was just a make-up date. Nothing more. And he had to remember that.

THE SUN BEGAN its descent toward the horizon, after several hours of enjoying the rides, the food, and learning more about each other. They made their way to the grandstands where the roping events were set to begin. Tyler paid for the tickets and led Georgia up to the seats that had the best view of the arena.

"Does your family live around here?" Georgia had hesitated to ask the question, but it had been on her mind all day. Now that they had a quiet moment as they waited for the rodeo to start, she broached the subject.

Tyler stiffened, pulling away from her slightly. "I don't have any family to speak of."

"What does that mean? Unless I'm sticking my nose where it doesn't belong." She paused, waiting to see if Tyler would explain further. While he was well-known as a cowboy for the Double H, nobody seemed to know anything more about him. At least, Ellen and Sam didn't know anything, except his reputation.

Tyler schooled his face. She wondered if Randall Hudson knew his story. If so, the owner of the sprawling ranch had kept it to himself.

"It's a long story. Look, they are getting ready to start." He pointed to the gate where the riders were gathering.

The announcer's voice blared just in time, quickly ending the conversation. Everyone stood for the national anthem. The rodeo queen blasted from the gate on her horse and circled the arena as fast as she could ride, the American flag flying from a pole held in one hand. The rider stopped in the center, while one of Georgia's students sang the anthem in a clear, beautiful voice. The anthem was followed by the Cowboy's Prayer.

Georgia had never been to a rodeo, so she had never heard the prayer before today. She listened in awe as many in the arena recited the prayer together, asking for safety for the cowboys, clean rides, and lives well-lived. It was inspiring. She looked up at Tyler who stood beside her with his hat in his hand and his head bowed, and smiled.

There were several events for today's rodeo. They began with the kids' events. Georgia cheered them on as they rode sheep, raced on little Shetland ponies, and chased goats with a chalk-filled dauber. Her eyes glittered with excitement as each boy or girl held their hands up high after catching their prize. She adored kids, and someday wanted a house full of them. She wondered how Tyler would be as a dad.

There were several more events as the adults took over. Barrel racers raced their horses around a pattern of three barrels, riding hard and fast to get the shortest time without knocking over any barrels.

Breakaway ropers sprung from gates in hot pursuit of a calf that ran from a different gate. The end of the rope was tied to the saddle horn by a small string. Once the rope tightened around the calf, the string would break, allowing the calf to escape.

All of these events were timed, and the fastest time took the prize. Georgia watched, first in fear for the calf, but then in amazement at the speed and agility of the riders.

Then it was time for Sam and his brother Rob to participate in the team roping event. They had been a duo since they began riding as kids and almost always came away as winners. Many said they could have made a decent living on the professional circuits.

"A record was set in San Antonio last year. Three point three seconds. Two full seconds faster than the leading team here, so far. So there is plenty of room for Sam and Rob." Tyler squeezed her hand, and she looked up at him briefly. Did he know her heart was pounding?

The gate opened to let the calf out and Sam and Rob began

the chase behind it. Georgia jumped away from Tyler and cheered, hands high in the air. Rob threw his rope over the calf's head, and Sam flicked his rope around one of the back heels. Their horses each backed up to pull the ropes tight, knowing exactly what to do. This was not a breakaway event. Poor calf. But it was over before it started, or almost. Four point nine seconds! Georgia cheered in triumph as Sam raised the cherished belt buckle, knocking off Tyler's hat as she lifted her hand in a wild wave.

"Oh, sorry." She grinned mischievously, and he smirked. He picked it up off the bench and plopped it on her head.

"There, that's better."

"Hm. It smells like you." *What does this mean? Is he really interested in me?* She wore it for a couple of minutes, then placed it back on his head. He had to have just been teasing.

Finally, it was time for the bull and bronc riders, who tried to stay on the wild twisting and bucking animals for eight seconds. It was a dangerous sport, and Georgia hid her eyes against Tyler's arm. He wrapped his arm around her and pulled her close, allowing her to peek out from where she hid her face against his chest. She heard the rumble that grew there as he chuckled and felt his heart under her cheek, beating as wildly as her own. Was it from the rodeo, or from their nearness? She decided to enjoy it for what it was. Two people sharing excitement together.

"That was fun! Don't you think so?" Georgia looked up at Tyler expecting to see his own elation over the events. Instead, she saw him staring intently at her. What was he thinking? Had she gone over the top with her enthusiasm?

"I think," Tyler said as he brushed a runaway strand of hair from her face. "I think you are the most beautiful thing I have ever seen." She thought for a heart-stopping moment he might kiss her. But instead, he tugged lightly at her ponytail again. The light action tugged on her heart.

Some might say that Tyler was flirting. But he looked completely serious to her. She hugged him tightly around his waist, hiding her eyes so he couldn't see what she was also feeling. This was only their second date. It was too soon to think serious thoughts.

Amos Carver took the stage just as the sun was setting behind the bleachers and the arena lights came on. The local band was one of Georgia's favorites. Their lead singer had a smooth Conway Twitty kind of vibe. When he sang "Hello, Darlin'," she almost melted. It was a warm and cozy feeling, lost in the music and the feel of two strong arms around her waist. But it was when they sang "Desperado," that she thought how perfectly it described the man by her side.

"I love this song." She sighed softly. It was a perfect night.

•——————•

TYLER WAS quiet as he drove Georgia home from the fair, his expression pinched. What was he thinking? She thought today had been fun.

"Tyler?"

He leaned his head toward her but kept his eyes on the road. "Hm?"

"You're being awfully quiet. Are you upset with me?"

"Just thinking. I have a lot of work to do tomorrow. We rotate weekend shifts, so I'm on duty."

"Oh." Tyler didn't elaborate any further, and Georgia didn't press him. She turned her head to look out the window at the stars overhead and they rode the rest of the way in silence.

They turned into her apartment complex and he parked in

one of the neighboring spaces. The curtain moved as they pulled up. The neighbor was peeking, of course. Tyler helped Georgia out of the truck and walked her to her door with his hand on her back.

"I had a really great time today. And tonight." Georgia looked up expectantly.

"I had a great time too. Thanks for going with me. Goodnight, Georgia." He placed his hands on either side of her face, his calluses rough as he smoothed his thumbs over her cheeks. Then he touched his lips to her cheek in a chaste kiss, and turned away, walking back to his truck.

Georgia slipped the key in her door as a tear slipped down her face. She watched him from the doorway as he climbed into his truck, backed out of the parking spot, and turned the vehicle toward the road. Shutting the door, she went to her window and slipped a corner of the curtain aside. Just like her neighbors were probably doing. And she let her tears fall.

●•—————————•●

TYLER COULD SEE the expectation in her eyes. It was all he could do to leave, but he had made a promise to Sam. It was an apology date. Nothing more.

Tyler tried to hide his thoughts with a poker face all the way home from the fair. Normally, at this stage in a date, he would have taken her to his favorite make-out spot. But it had been a long day, and Georgia wasn't a good-time filly. Georgia was different. Special. And she deserved to be treated that way.

He swallowed hard. His truck carried her scent of honeysuckle, mingled with fried food on the night breeze. He recalled floating over the midway on the Ferris wheel, visiting the exhibits, and enjoying brisket sandwiches together. The scrambling ride was the highlight. Her laughter filled his ears as they spun in crazy circles. But it was her nearness, pressed up against him as she was, that spun circles around his heart. The memory almost did him in. He wanted to turn around and kiss her properly, but he was determined to be a gentleman. *Just keep walking.*

The diesel engine rumbled as he prepared to leave, his headlights illuminating her doorway as she stepped through into the safety of her apartment. He thought he saw her wipe away a tear. It must have been his imagination. Or a trick of the darkness. The beams of light swept the apartment building as he backed out of the space. He sat there for a full second, took a deep breath, and began his drive back to the ranch.

Flipping on his radio that was tuned to a country station, he was surprised to hear the Eagle's oldie. "Desperado." And as he sat his beat-up black hat on his dresser to turn in for the night, the song continued to plague him. He had no business pursuing her. She was all the queens in the deck wrapped up in one quirky, beautiful, fun, and way too good for him woman. And he would forever want the one he couldn't get.

# SIX

GEORGIA WAS FOLLOWED around at church all Sunday morning by people with smiles, nods, and general curiosity. She hadn't had this much attention since she fell into the creek two years ago and came to church with a black eye. It was one date, for Pete's sake, and she didn't even remember seeing most of these people at the fair, but word must have spread. Their I-know-what-you-did-last-night expressions made her cringe. They didn't know any such thing.

She thought about the day they had spent together, reviewing it in her mind while the preacher talked about loving your neighbor. Tyler had been quiet as they had toured through the butterfly display, keeping his thoughts to himself, even while guiding her with his hand lightly at her waist. He frowned when they looked at the moths. She admitted they were not the most beautiful bug in the world, but she was curious about what he was thinking when he jerked back as a moth flew toward the window, smacking into it before flying away.

The quilts were beautiful. She could have stayed there all

day. But Tyler was not interested, so they went back to the midway where they had enjoyed the ride. The scrambling ride had pushed them together and she had nearly landed in his lap. She blushed at the thought, but then the preacher said something a bit loudly, his eyes on her, bringing her attention back to the sermon.

After the service, Ellen pulled her through the parking lot to her car.

"You were lost there for a moment during the service. Where did your mind go?"

Georgia hated to tell her sister what she had been thinking, but Ellen's keen eye focused on her as if she knew.

"Come to my house for lunch. We can catch up there, and you can tell me all about Mr. Tall Black Hat Guy. I'll make Sam go out to grab some barbeque and we can talk then, without him around."

Georgia sighed. There wasn't really much to tell, but that wouldn't make any difference. It was a simple day at the fair, a chaste kiss on the cheek, and then he left. Just like that. No "I'll call you," or even a "See ya around." He just left.

Georgia shook her head as she recalled the night with her sister, leaving out some of the details. She should have known not to expect more. Sam had told her that Tyler wanted to apologize. And he had. But she hadn't known how her heart would thump as she leaned next to him during the concert. She hadn't known how warm she would feel inside with his arms around her. She hadn't known that her cheek would tingle from the barest of touches from his lips, how his scent would linger on the jacket she had worn. She hadn't known how deeply she would be affected, and how she would ache to see him again. And it hadn't even been twenty-four hours since he left her at her door.

"Ellen, what was it like when you and Sam fell in love?"

Ellen looked quizzically at her little sister. "Don't tell me you think you are in love with Tyler. You have been out with him twice, and the first time was a disaster."

"No, that's not it. I was just wondering. Did you know at first that there was a connection between you two? Or did it take time?" She drew circles on the eat-in kitchen table with her finger.

Ellen leaned back against the kitchen counter. "I actually thought Sam was a jerk when I first met him. You know. Big man on campus and all. Conceited. Arrogant. He had some kind of roping scholarship, and everyone said he would turn pro."

"What happened?" Georgia had never heard this story.

"I was sitting outside the student union building one day. He and some friends were practicing their roping skills on some dummies that were set up on the lawn there. He threw the rope, and it landed around me."

Georgia sighed. "That sounds so romantic."

"It was anything but. I was furious. So he offered to buy me an ice cream cone, and it kind of took off from there." Ellen speared Georgia with a look. "Tell me, is there a you and Tyler? Sam won't like that."

"Yeah, I guess he is still that conceited, arrogant guy, isn't he?" Georgia wiggled her eyebrows at Ellen. "Besides, there is no me and Tyler."

Tomorrow was Monday. She would go back to her students, and he would go back to pushing cattle around on the ranch. He would move on to other women and probably never think of her again. She would remember him forever.

•—————•

TYLER RODE ten miles of fence line, inspecting and fixing where needed. It took him away from the jabs, ribs, and "what was she like" comments from the other cowboys on the ranch, but it also gave him way too much time to think. He wasn't about to kiss and tell. Not this time. But there really wasn't that much to tell. She was soft, sweet, and wonderful, and he didn't deserve her. And he hadn't even kissed her.

He leaned over the saddle horn, resting his forearm on top, the reins hanging lightly from his fingers, and looked out over the expanse of grass, dotted by cattle and an occasional tree. Texas Hill Country was not dry and dusty like the western half of the state. The grass waved gracefully in the breeze, green and luscious. The herd munched lazily, oblivious to the world around them. This was why he was a cowboy. He understood the mindset of the person that had written "Home on the Range." He didn't have a house or condo like most people. He was at home in the saddle. There was a peace here on the range that couldn't be found anywhere else on earth.

His thoughts wandered back to Georgia, and the peace was gone. He had walked away from her abruptly after escorting her to her door. He thought his heart would burst, but it was better this way. He was just like that poor moth, smacking into the window without even knowing what had hit him.

Her wavy, auburn hair was silky under his chin as she laid her head back against his chest during the concert. He didn't even remember what her hair felt like on that first date. He had focused on the physical attraction to her, but hadn't really seen her.

But Saturday, he noticed the green of her eyes, the dimple in her left cheek when she smiled, the soft way she ordered those frozen ice cream dots at the fair, and the dainty way she ate them, one small spoonful at a time. They played the mole whacking game and she was surprisingly good, winning against him every time. He would have to remember that aggressive tendency.

Moving further up the fence line, he found a honeysuckle vine growing around one of the posts, its trumpet-shaped yellow flowers hanging full on the vine. It wound its way up the post and along the wire, invading his heart with its sweet aroma. He had remembered that sweet smell all night after the fair. He also recalled the fire in her eyes from their first date when she had told him in no uncertain terms that she would not be "one of his conquests." She was already a notch on his heart, if he was being honest.

He spent Monday night at a line shack on the far side of the ranch after riding several miles inspecting the fences. He found that Cap's company was far better than that of the other ranch hands. The chestnut-colored Quarter Horse was a solid, steady companion. His ears would twitch forward and back, listening. Sometimes, he would turn his head back toward Tyler as they rode together, as if to say, *"Are you nuts?"* But mostly, his response to Tyler's ramblings was a soft nicker.

It was clear that Georgia liked kids. Would she want a house full of her own someday? Did he? Kids may be in his future, but right now, he didn't even have a home. What would that home look like? What would his kids look like? Would they look like him? Or like Georgia?

He rolled onto his side and closed his eyes, wishing for the night sounds to lull him to sleep. He would finish riding the fence line tomorrow. Hopefully by then his bunkmates will have found something else to talk about. But when he fell asleep, he saw green eyes and butterflies. Right before he smashed head-first into a windshield.

GEORGIA WALKED INTO HER CLASSROOM, set her backpack on the chair next to her desk, and took out her laptop as her students filed into the room. Several kids looked at her and snickered behind their hands, but she thought nothing of it. They were, after all, eighth graders. Then Emily Harris, called Saucy by her friends, walked straight up to her desk and asked what was apparently the question of the day. "Miss Duncan, did you really go out with Tyler?" She didn't even have to say his last name. Everyone in Nora Hills knew who Tyler was.

As if that was anybody's business. But it was definitely not her students' business.

Rather than answer Emily's question directly, she complimented the girl. "I was at the fair watching Sam and Rob win the team roping event. You did a beautiful job with the national anthem, by the way. You have a lovely voice."

"Thanks, Miss Duncan." Emily turned and looked at two other girls with an I-told-you-so smirk. All three nodded seriously and made notes in their notebooks. It made Georgia's stomach turn sour. She wanted her students to respect her. Not to be spreading calculating rumors.

# SEVEN

IT HAD BEEN a couple of weeks since Georgia had seen Tyler. He truly was gone. She hadn't even seen him on the street, and Sam hadn't seen him picking up ranch supplies at the Farm and Ranch Store. Today she and Ellen were shopping at the local big box store, stocking up on household items that they would split and share. Baby Sam Junior was tucked into his car seat in the cart, surrounded by diapers and bulk food items.

A large brown truck drove up another aisle as they walked through the parking lot to Ellen's SUV. Georgia followed the truck with her eyes, but it wasn't him.

"He must have made quite an impact on you."

Georgia turned to Ellen. She knew who her older sister was talking about and didn't even try to argue. "Not really. Just noticed the truck." But her heart was saying something else.

There were two ways out of the parking lot. She saw the Double H ranch truck in another aisle, moving toward the main exit, where there was more room to maneuver the large vehicle. They met at the exit to the highway and Georgia looked into the cab to find Tyler staring directly at her. He ducked his head and pulled through the intersection. She couldn't keep the hurt from her face.

He had purposely ignored her. Pure and simple.

"You were right. He was here. Just not in his truck." Ellen said the words that Georgia didn't want to say.

Georgia turned her face toward the window, away from Ellen. She didn't want her sister to see her tears.

"Hey. Are you okay? Tell me, what really happened after you guys left the fair? I know you are aware of the rumors. How much of what is floating around is true?" Ellen reached out to touch Georgia's arm before putting her hand back on the steering wheel.

"None of it is true. I promise you." Georgia finally turned back to Ellen.

"Then why are you crying?" Ellen's voice was soft, like the voice she used when trying to shush her crying baby. Ellen pulled through the intersection, onto the highway.

"He was so sweet. I thought for just a moment we might have connected. But I guess I was wrong." Georgia wiped a tear from her cheek.

"You really like him, don't you?"

Georgia twisted in her seat, turning fully to Ellen. "There's something about him that's vulnerable. Like he's searching for something and doesn't know what it is. I guess maybe I want to help him find that something."

Ellen placed her hand on Georgia's shoulder. "You can't fix him, Georgia. You know that. It's a classic blunder made by nearly every woman alive."

Georgia sighed and turned to look out the window again, biting her thumbnail as she did. She thought that maybe God would use her to help Tyler. But maybe she was wrong. She knew you should never expect to change a guy. That was many young ladies' biggest mistake, and a source for many broken hearts. So why was she so upset?

•————————•

TYLER SPOTTED Georgia as he drove through the parking lot. He had borrowed the ranch truck because his was in the shop getting new brakes and other normal maintenance. He stopped to let a car back out of a parking spot and used the opportunity to watch her from the safe distance. Her auburn hair was pulled back into her normal high ponytail, her jeans fit nicely over her slim hips. She had glanced over at the other brown diesel dually, then turned back to Ellen with a look of disappointment on her face.

He couldn't tell what they were saying, but his ears burned as if they were talking about him. The car in front of him pulled away and he continued around toward the exit. His fingers itched to hit the call button on the truck's Bluetooth system, but he held back, tapping his thumb on the steering wheel instead.

Lately, he had been staying away from town. His cohorts accused him of hiding out on the ranch, and his boss had finally told him to take the ranch truck and "go do something" for the day. He was grumpy, and he knew it.

What was that old Scottish quote again? "If wishes were horses, beggars would ride."

If only.

•————————•

"THERE IS a full moon Friday night. It's supposed to be the

Super Pink Moon. Wanna' come watch it with me? I know a place out on the ranch that has a killer view."

Tyler's finger twitched when he hit the send button. He waited for her response, wondering if she would make him wait until the end of the school day. But then his phone chimed.

"What time?" The response came so fast, the special chime he had set for her on his phone startled him.

"Moonrise starts early but it peaks at ten thirty. I'll pick you up at eight."

"Okay."

Tyler had tried to forget her. But every time he closed his eyes, he saw her sparkling emerald orbs dancing before him. All he wanted was one more night with her. A chance to talk and get to know her. No strings attached. He figured watching the moon rise over Nora Hills would be a good way to do that. Hopefully, he would be witty enough to make her laugh. That should be easy to do, right?

Tyler picked Georgia up at eight on the dot. She was dressed in jeans and a purple blouse and covered that with another purple sweater, since the night air might be a little cool. Her signature ponytail swayed from side to side as she climbed into his truck with Tyler's assistance once again. Tyler, of course, was in his typical plaid shirt, jeans, and boots. He had also brought along a denim jacket. He touched the small of her back as she exited her apartment, shutting the door behind her and checking to make sure it was locked.

They drove up to the hill as the sun was starting to set. Tyler parked his truck so that the tailgate faced to the northeast, where the moon would rise. He didn't plan it as a romantic date, just a "get to know you" time of friendship. He had packed a cooler of her favorite designer iced tea, along with some cheese, apples, grapes, and crackers.

The sky turned from dusk into night while a whippoorwill

sang softly. Georgia saw the first star, and one by one they popped out as the sky grew darker. Soon, the moon made its appearance on the eastern horizon, and a hush fell between them as they watched the sky's nighttime show. Katydids and crickets accompanied the moon's appearance, their chirps blending together in musical harmony.

Looking up became difficult as the moon rose higher into the sky. He hadn't packed chairs to sit in and mentally kicked himself, thinking it might have been a good idea. Instead, they sat on the tailgate, which also became hard to sit on. Tyler watched as Georgia shifted, trying to stay comfortable.

"Is this tailgate getting hard?"

Georgia rocked her hips from side to side and smiled softly. "Yeah, it is. But that's okay. I'm enjoying just being here."

Tyler picked up her hand and rubbed it gently before releasing it. He hadn't touched her at all tonight, except to help her onto the tailgate. He was even careful to keep his fingers from touching hers as he handed her the bottle of tea. But he wanted to extend this date just a little bit longer. He breathed in deeply, taking in her sweet smell.

"I have a couple of sleeping bags in the crew cab. I sometimes use one when I go out to the more remote areas of the ranch and know I'm going to be there overnight. If you want, I can get them out and we can spread them over the bed of the truck. Maybe they will help cushion the ridges in the truck bed. There is also a blanket there that we can use for a pillow. That should be a little bit more comfortable for us to look up, if you would like to stay a little bit more. Is that okay?"

He grinned when she said yes. She slid from the tailgate to the truck bed, leaning against the blanket he had rolled into a pillow, and he gave her another small blanket that was just big enough for one, which she immediately snuggled under. Texas nights in the springtime could get chilly, in spite of the heat of the day.

Feeling like a giddy teenager, he couldn't stop himself. He reached for her hand, and she placed her smaller one in his, linking their fingers as she did so. When he glanced sideways, he found a small smile twitching on the corner of her mouth. It gave him courage.

Tyler got as close as he dared while still leaving space between them. He really wanted to respect her this time. They watched as the moon glided through the night sky, the stars twinkling around it. They even saw a shooting star, which burned bright and fast, and then just as quickly flamed out. Was that what this relationship would be? Over before it started? He hoped not.

The moon grew brighter as the sky grew darker. It was so large it felt like you could reach out and touch it. And Tyler knew then that if he could pluck it from the sky and present it to Georgia as a gift, he would.

There were a few lights in the valley below them, mostly from the guest house and cabins. The rest of the area was covered in inky blackness, making the sky seem brighter and allowing them to watch the constellations as they moved from east to west. Occasionally, they heard sounds from restless cows mooing into the night.

Tyler checked the time on his phone. The moon had peaked and he knew they would have to leave soon. Inwardly, he promised himself another thirty minutes and he would take her home.

*"When I look up into the heavens and see the stars and all that you made there, I think Who am I that you are mindful of me?"* Georgia spoke aloud, but not to Tyler.

"Hm? What does that mean?" Tyler played with her fingers as he held her hand.

"It is so lovely out here, it reminds me of that Bible verse. It's from Psalm 8. That God made us and everything around us." She turned more fully to him. "We are fearfully and wonderfully made. That's from Psalm 139. Did you know that? Take the moon for instance. It is so fascinating. I read that it is at the closest point to the Earth in its orbit, which is why it looks so much bigger tonight than other nights. And we mean more to God than even the moon." She turned her head to say something else, and she was close enough that if he wanted to, he could brush his lips across hers.

He wanted to kiss her. He had promised himself he would keep the date friendly. But then she snuggled next to him, so he put his arm around her. They both grew quiet again as they watched the moon and the stars glide through the night sky, enjoying the peace that came with it.

# EIGHT

TYLER'S PHONE buzzed in his pocket, and he reached for it to turn his alarm off. It must be five a.m. and time to. . .

"Holy Cow Patties!"

The night sky was just starting to turn the shade of blue that made him think of sapphires just before dawn. Georgia tried to get up, and they realized they were twisted together under the blanket. She shoved at him to escape the cocoon of warmth and embarrassment. The more they tried to escape the blanket, the more tangled it became around them.

"Georgia! I am so sorry! We must have fallen asleep." He swore under his breath. "Oh, crud. I need to take you home. Hold still while I unwrap the blanket." He tugged at it, trying to pull the ends free. "How did it get this way?" He ran his hand through his thick hair. "Your sister and brother-in-law are going to kill me."

"It's not any more your fault than it is mine. Did you know she wanted to put a tracking app on my phone?" Georgia shook her head as she recalled the conversation in her mind. "I told her I trust you. And I could take care of myself. Let's pack everything up. And I promise I'll explain everything to them."

It was five-thirty when Tyler pulled into the parking lot of Georgia's apartment complex. He knew his truck was loud and had a distinctive sound, so he stopped near the entrance. He hated that she would have to walk, but he thought it was more important that people didn't see her getting out of his truck at this time in the morning.

"You might as well take me to my door. I have nothing to hide."

"Are you sure?" He glanced sideways at her, wary.

"Yes. I'm a grown woman, and I have done nothing to be ashamed of."

Tyler watched the curtains of the apartments on both sides of hers fall as she got out of his truck. The older ladies had seen her coming in. Don't they ever sleep?

When he walked into the bunkhouse a half hour later, Reggie raised an eyebrow. Tyler glared back at Reggie, daring him to say something. He burned with frustration, knowing that his actions would have serious consequences. But Georgia had said she would explain everything to Sam and Ellen. All he could do was wait for the fallout. He knew there would be consequences to pay.

•◦————————◦•

"WHERE WERE YOU LAST NIGHT?" Ellen stood in Georgia's apartment at ten o'clock that morning, arms folded across her chest. Sam was just behind her, thunder clouds gathering in his eyes. The baby slept peacefully in his car seat, unaware of the storm that was brewing around him.

"What do you mean?" Georgia tried her most innocent look.

"I sent at least five text messages to you last night. And called you twice. You didn't respond, so we got worried and came over. Your car was here, but you weren't."

Georgia held her chin up. "I went on a date. I had my phone on silent and wasn't checking it. It was the respectful thing to do." Georgia didn't mean to sound defensive, but she felt like she was under attack.

"We knocked on your door. When you didn't answer, one of your neighbors said you left with Tyler. This morning, she called and said she saw him drop you off. At five-thirty. You want to tell us what happened?"

Now Ellen was tapping her foot. Sheesh. You'd think she was her mother.

"Oh, for Pete's sake! I am a grown woman and can do what I want. But for the record, we went out to watch the pink moon. It got late, and we fell asleep." Why did they think she needed to kiss and tell? Actually, he hadn't even kissed her.

Ellen groaned and looked up at the ceiling before looking back at Georgia. "Oh, honey, you didn't!"

Sam raised his hands in frustration. "You slept with him?"

"No! I did not sleep with him. We fell asleep. There is a difference." Georgia gave Sam a defiant look, hands on her hips.

"Where did you go?" Ellen's questioning was definitely accusatory.

"We went to a hilltop there on the ranch. It was a great place to watch the moon. It was really cool, this big giant ball in the sky, larger than I have ever seen it." She held her hands up, indicating how large the moon had looked. Maybe that would deflect the conversation.

Sam huffed. "You went to his hilltop?" His brown eyes turned black with the insinuation.

"What do you mean by *his* hilltop? It's on Hudson ranch property." Georgia dropped her hands, confused.

Ellen took Georgia's hand and tugged her toward the couch, softening her voice. "Georgia, that's where Tyler takes all his girls."

Georgia furrowed her eyebrows and looked at Ellen. Then at Sam, then back at Ellen. She swallowed hard, tears forming puddles in her eyes.

"What do you mean, *all his girls?*" Her eyes scrunched in pain as she considered the implications of that statement. "How do you know about his dating habits?" Georgia was perturbed. She didn't listen to town gossip, but apparently her sister did.

"Yes, Georgia. All his girls. Guys talk, you know. And now you will likely be a subject in those conversations." Sam tempered his look, but he was obviously boiling inside.

Georgia didn't tell Ellen that she woke up to find herself wrapped in Tyler's arms. Tightly. In fact, they were quite snug, her head on his chest, his hand resting possessively on her lower hip, her leg tucked between his. Stuck together within the warmth of the blanket.

Ellen's eyes became wary. "What did you have to drink? Is it possible he put something in your drink?"

"No, that's not possible." Georgia was shocked. The bottle of designer sweet tea had been sealed so tightly she couldn't get it open. He had to do it for her, which in retrospect caused her to pause. Had he really put something in her drink? Would he have done that? She thought she knew him by now, but maybe she didn't know him well enough to be sure one way or the other.

TUESDAY MORNING, Tyler was walking out of the Farm and Ranch Store while Sam was walking in. Sam turned on his heel and called to Tyler. "Grant!"

Tyler turned around, just as Sam's fist smashed into his face. He fell backwards into a pile of bagged mulch, his hat flying several feet to the side. Tyler struggled to regain his balance. He wiped his mouth with the back of his hand, finding blood and snot, and hoped his nose wasn't broken. He reached into his back pocket for a handkerchief and couldn't find it, so he wiped his face again using his sleeve.

Tyler glared into Sam's face and found a swirling tornado of anger. The threat of another fist ready to strike. He decided on honesty.

"I guess I deserved that."

Sam swore. "Darn right, Grant, you deserved it. I told you not to hurt her." Sam never swore, which indicated how angry he was. Tyler felt like he was sitting on a nest of fire ants.

"Can we take this conversation somewhere less public?" Tyler looked around and waved his hand, indicating the crowd that had gathered to gawk. "We didn't do anything. I didn't do anything."

Sam was hurting Georgia more by making this a public spectacle. He stood over Tyler and lowered his voice to a crawl, his brows furrowed, finger pointed in Tyler's face, the menacing words clear. "You stayed out all night watching the moon. From the back of your truck. And fell asleep. Together. Under a blanket. In your special spot. Where you take all your girls. And you say you didn't 'do anything?'" He punctuated his last words with air quotes.

Sam picked up Tyler's hat from the pavement and tossed it at him. "Georgia is too naïve for you, Tyler. Stay away from her." Then he walked away, leaving the gawkers to stare. He didn't even go back into the store.

Tyler hadn't thought about the implication of taking Georgia to that spot on the hill. He just knew it was a good place to watch the moon. Now he groaned at what he had done. He really hadn't intended for this to happen. He pulled himself off the stack of mulch bags, found the handkerchief in his other pocket, and wiped the dried blood off his face before walking to his truck. He may not have fully thought out the date. But Sam was wrong about one thing. Georgia wasn't naïve. She was pure.

# NINE

GEORGIA PICKED up her keys and phone and stuck each into a hip pocket. Ellen was meeting her at the Blue Bull and had driven separately so she could get back early to Sam and the baby. It would be good to get out, and the Blue Bull had a mean Sunrise Cheeseburger—with bacon, dandelion greens, and a runny quail egg on top. It was terribly fattening, but enjoying the juicy burger and crunchy fries was a luxury she gave herself once in a while.

Two hours later, darkness had fallen and the lights twinkled over the deck where they enjoyed their outdoor meal. Ellen had left thirty minutes ago, but Georgia stayed to enjoy the music from their table on the deck. She had also spent much of that time thinking about Tyler and arguing with herself. She and Ellen had discussed the cowboy at length. Ellen said she could do better. Georgia thought Ellen should butt out.

Tin Top Highway was on stage. She wove her way through the indoor tables surrounding the dance floor, stopped by the restroom with the pink boot on the door, washed her hands, then made her way back through the crowd, getting almost to the exit when a pair of arms grabbed her from behind and swung her around.

"Hey, darlin'. How's about a little two-steppin'?" The slur in his voice was telling, along with the longneck in his hand. That dust devil sucked her right in.

Georgia started to push back but wasn't quick enough. Before she knew it, she was swirling around the dance floor. She looked up at the gray eyes under the black hat and wasn't sure he even knew who she was.

"You're drunk, Tyler."

Tyler pulled her in even tighter. "Yep. I'm drunk. Dance with me, darlin'." He wrapped his arms around her, pulling her head to his chest. The song switched to a slow melody, and he stood there with her in the middle of the dance floor, swaying back and forth. She smelled of honeysuckle. He smelled of beer.

"You need to go home. How did you get here?" She looked up into his face and spread her hands across his plaid shirt. She tried to keep her arms between them. He was too solid.

"Don' have a ride. Reggie lef' wif some chick. So it's jus' you and me, an' ev'rybody else here." Tyler waved one arm at the crowd, then pulled it tight around her waist again, initiating more swirls that made her dizzy. She wondered how he could even stand.

The bar was crowded. Most of the people there knew Tyler, or at least knew about his escapades. Nobody was going to step in. They figured that Georgia was okay with the way he was holding her. The look on her face must have been euphoric. Or maybe dumbfounded. It was hard to tell which way she was feeling.

Georgia eventually maneuvered Tyler to a booth, where they were able to sit down across from each other. A waitress picked up the empty bottle. Georgia tried to order a cup of coffee for him, but he pushed the cup away with a silly grin. He had both elbows on the table, his head leaning against one hand in a cockeyed fashion, eyes glassy, with streaks of red running through them.

"Don' wan' no coffee. Wan' you." He walked his fingers across the table toward her, flicking her hand with his index finger when he reached hers.

"Did you know," his Texas drawl mixed with his slur, "your eyes look like di'mons? No, wait, make that em'ralds. You could take a million stars, and they still wouldn' sparkle the way your eyes do when you're mad. Like righ' now." His lips slid into a silly grin.

Georgia rolled her eyes. She wouldn't fall for it. All the flattery in the world could not make her sorry for him, especially after all the talk about their last time together. His eyes were glazed over as he tried to focus. His elbow slipped on the table, and he struggled to put it back in place.

"Sorry, Tyler," Georgia said. "Pretty words won't work tonight. But since Reggie abandoned you, I guess I'll have to get you home." Tyler leered at her, leaning closer over the table. The beer on his breath was strong. How long had he been drinking?

Georgia looked around. The bartender was on the other side of the room serving a table full of rowdy cowboys. She thought about calling Sam, but Ellen had left to go home, and she didn't want to interrupt their night. She could call the ranch, but that might get him into trouble, although they surely knew of his habits. Sighing, she decided that she would have to be the one to take him home.

Tyler had his arm around Georgia's shoulder as they left the bar. She did her best to support him, but she was a foot shorter than he was. He tipped his hat with his other hand as a group of young ladies entered the bar, and almost dropped it. The girls giggled.

She steered the cowboy toward her stink bug, as he had called it that first day, and watched him try to fold himself into it. He didn't quite fit. Even with the seat pushed back as far as it would go, his head bumped the headliner, and that was without his hat, which he held in his hands. His knees bent awkwardly. It would be an uncomfortable ride to the ranch, which was fifteen miles away.

Georgia started the engine and slid another look sideways at Tyler. He was starting to turn the color of her car. She lowered his window using the button on her door. Maybe the cool night air would keep him from heaving everywhere. Making a snap decision against her better judgment, she pulled out of the parking lot, steering away from the ranch, and drove the other direction to her apartment, which was closer. At least it was on the ground floor, and her designated parking spot was just a few feet from her door.

She unlocked and opened her front door first, then helped Tyler from her car. She leaned him next to the hood to close the car door, then took his arm and held it around her shoulder with one hand, her other arm around his waist.

They barely made it to her couch before he fell, face-first onto the seat. She grunted as she picked up his legs, one boot at a time, and swung each onto the cushion. His feet stuck out over the end. Finding his hat on the floor, she placed it on her dining table. Finally, she closed and locked her front door, turned and walked into her bedroom, closed that door, and locked it with a resounding click.

She leaned her back against the door and squeezed her face between her hands.

"What have I done?"

TYLER WAS STARTLED by a thump on his head, followed by something tickling his ear. His head buzzed as he struggled to orient himself, but his brain was not responding. He reached his arm over his head to swat at the offending thing, smacking away something furry. At least he thought it was furry. The buzzing stopped, and he wondered if he had imagined it.

Soft green light glowed from somewhere, giving him enough light to see shapes, but not much else. He looked around at the unfamiliar room, wondering where he was and how he had gotten there.

"What have I done now?" The groan came from his own lips, and he cringed with the possible consequence of his actions. He patted his body, thankful that he was not in a state of undress. That was a relief. But he still didn't know where he was, or how he got there. He had a brief memory of dancing with Georgia. Was that just a dream? He closed his eyes again, squeezing them tight.

The sound of feet tiptoeing across the floor woke him again. Or maybe it was the sun shining through the cracks in the slatted blinds behind the sheer curtains. He opened one eye, saw Georgia's face peering down at him, and quickly shut it. Sam would slug him again. He was sure of it.

Georgia poured two cups of coffee and placed them on the dining table. She left the room for a few minutes before returning, her expression determined.

Standing next to the couch, she prodded him none too gently. "Good morning, sleepy head." The words were not exactly angry, but her tone said differently. She grabbed both of his arms and pulled him into a sitting position, swinging his legs off the couch. The look on her face reminded him of the one his grandmother used to make before switching his rear for some offense or another.

"I made coffee for you." Pointing to the dining table, she indicated he should move to the seat where she sat one of the mugs. His hat was sitting next to one of them. He wished she would just yell at him. No, that would make his head hurt. His troubles were of his own making, and she wasn't responsible for him. So why had she brought him here last night?

A cat sat on a carpeted tree, the calico staring at him from her perch in front of the window. Was that what had landed on his head earlier? He didn't like cats. They were great for keeping mice out of grain bins, but were constantly under foot, rubbing against his legs and tripping him as he walked.

Looking back at it warily, he got up from the couch and groaned on his way to the table before finally shifting his gaze to Georgia. Between the gravity of the situation, the gravity making him wobbly, and one of the worst hangovers of his life, he was afraid to open his mouth. He didn't know what to say, anyway. What had happened last night? And how did he end up on Georgia's couch? He didn't think they had done anything inappropriate, but he didn't know for sure.

"Where's your truck? I'll take you back to get it." Her look was stern, reminding him of his third-grade teacher after he had swiped another kid's hat off his head and plunked it on his own. He bet that look helped keep her class in line.

He shook his head, trying to clear his brain, but that was a mistake. "I don't know. I don't remember much of what happened last night, and I'm sorry. But I don't think I drove. I went to the bar with Reggie and then . . . I think he left but I'm not sure."

Tyler squinted as he tried to remember, but he kept his eyes focused downward toward the table, his hands clasped around the mug in front of him. He swallowed hard, his Adam's apple sliding up and down his throat as he did. Then something occurred to him.

"Why were you there last night?" He started to come out of his fog.

"At the Blue Bull?"

"Yeah. That's not your normal hangout place."

Georgia shifted in her seat. "I met Ellen there. She needed a break from the baby so we had a girl's night out. But then Sam called and she left early. So I stayed for a while to listen to the music. I was leaving, and almost out the door when you snagged me from behind."

Tyler processed what she had just said. Another minute and he would have missed her, but she wouldn't have had to deal with him.

"Yeah, I'm sorry about that. I hope I didn't inconvenience you." He tapped his hat where it sat on the table.

"Inconvenience me?" Georgia scoffed and looked at him with wide, angry eyes. She stood abruptly, making him jump, his head pounding harder. "You accost me in the bar, force me to dance with you, practically puke in my car, bring your stinky body into my home where you fall flat onto my couch, and now I'm going to have to take you home. And I'm going to miss church service. And I was supposed to sing this morning. And all you can say is that you hope you didn't inconvenience me?"

"Church?" *She sings?*

Her voice was musical, a comforting song with each breath, each word, as long as she wasn't shouting. He looked up at her from the coffee cup that had become his anchor right now. She was going to have one of those meltdown things that women sometimes do. And he didn't know how to handle that.

"Um, accost you?" He rested his forehead on his hand. It seemed he had a lot of sins to pay for today. "What did I do?"

She was silent for a heartbeat, so he continued. "Why did

you bring me here? You could have left me there at the bar. Or called a ride share. The bartender, Jeff, would have called someone at the ranch to come and get me." He paused and looked down at his cup, embarrassed in front of her. "He's done that before."

"I don't know why I brought you here. I guess I . . ." She sighed, waving her hand in the air before rubbing her own forehead. "I don't know why."

Her phone beeped. He saw Ellen's name on the screen before she typed a quick response.

"I'll call Reggie." Tyler pulled his phone from his hip pocket. It was a miracle it was still there.

"No, I'll take you."

"You're gonna be late for church."

She sighed. "I'm already late. Church started at nine."

Tyler checked his phone. It was nine-thirty.

He was humbled by Georgia's assistance. He honestly didn't remember doing any of the things she said he did. And yet, she had brought him to her home to let him sleep it off. He gulped the last drop of his coffee, snatched his hat off the table, and set it on his head. Her neighbors on each side peered through their curtains as they left the apartment together. Pulling his hat low, he hid his eyes from the glare of the sunlight and the glares from her neighbors. He had obviously spent the night there. Now the rumors really would fly.

• •————————• •

THE SILENCE in the car was not pleasant, on top of the fact that he was folded up like a pretzel. Tyler struggled for something to say that would break the tension.

76

"Sing something for me." Maybe that would help. "What were you supposed to sing today? Sing it for me. Please."

Georgia glanced at him sideways, keeping her face toward the road. "Are you serious? You want me to sing to you?"

"I know I've caused you a lot of trouble. But I would love to hear you sing."

"I don't have any music."

"Do you need music?"

"Well, no."

"Good. This way I can hear your voice. You know I like good music." He wiggled his eyebrows before closing his eyes in pain. He couldn't wait for this hangover to fade.

Georgia cleared her throat. Tyler waited in anticipation for another speech, but widened his eyes in surprise as she began to sing.

Her voice was as crystal clear as his grandmother's wind chimes. Tyler was entranced. He could understand why she would sing at church. He remembered hearing his grandmother sing this song about a garden when he was a small boy. The words were low and soothing.

*And he walks with me and he talks with me*
*And he tells me I am his own*
*And the joy we share as we tarry there*
*None other has ever known.*

She had a beautiful voice, reminding him of someone famous he had once seen in concert. He knew the song Georgia sang was about Jesus. He remembered that much from when he went to church as a kid with his family. But it also seemed like a song about love and fidelity and it made him feel a bit guilty. He wouldn't know the meaning of either. He wondered if she could ever sing a song like that about him.

# TEN

HYPOCRITE.

That was the newest gossip that had been going around about her for the past week. Hanging out at the bars at night, taking cowboys home with her, then going to church the next morning. Or not going, as in this case. What would her parents say if they were still alive? The Girl Next Door, everybody's favorite goody-two-shoes, was just another party girl.

Georgia could imagine the whispers. She knew the church was gossiping about her. But when she got to school the next day, she saw the shadowed glances from the other teachers. Students whispered behind their hands in the hallway and turned away as she walked by. How had she gotten herself into this mess? Some of the girls made notes about her on their social media accounts, feeding the rumor mill. Or at least that is what she heard when they whispered together.

*Why, oh why, hadn't she just taken him to the ranch? Then again, plenty of people had seen them leaving together. Would it have made any difference?*

Her phone pinged with an incoming message. Ellen was checking on her. She sent back a quick reply.

"Can we get together to talk? Maybe after school today?"

"I assume this is about Tyler?"

"Ellen, what am I going to do?"

"Hey. It will be okay. I'm just getting the baby down for a nap. Come on over and we will talk through it together."

Hopefully, Ellen can help calm her nerves. But then, what?

•————————•

"I'M GONNA KILL HIM." Figuratively, of course. Sam had promised Tyler that if he hurt Georgia, there would be a reckoning.

"We didn't do anything, Sam."

"That's not what I'm hearing."

Georgia thought it would just be herself and Ellen, but Sam had come home early, stomping as he came in through the back door. He slammed his hat down on the kitchen table, then sat and pulled off his muddy boots. Why were they muddy? Must have been a hard day, which wouldn't help her situation, at all.

"I helped some guys with a broken water line over at the V&B Ranch. It was all they could talk about. That you were seen leaving the Blue Bull with Tyler, and he was pretty drunk. Then you put him in your car—I don't know how, it is so small —and left together. And you know what they were insinuating? It was all I could do not to bust a few heads."

"I just told you, we didn't do anything. If we had, I would understand why you would be so mad. But I barely got him into my apartment as it was. I don't know why I took him home with me. I think I just saw someone in need."

"Your apartment. Really? Because he was someone in need? Would you do that with any cowboy who swings you across the dance floor and says he needs you?" Sam's dark eyes glared, icy in response. "How am I supposed to defend you if you continue to act this way?"

Georgia glared back. Turning to Ellen, she raised her hands in frustration. "Is that what you think of me?" Tears slipped down her face. She had hoped they would understand.

Ellen reached her hand across the table to Georgia's. "Honey, it's not what *we* think." She gave Sam the evil eye. "But it does appear to have been another lapse in judgement on your part. We are concerned for you and the gossip that is going around. We don't want you hurting, whether because of Tyler or because of what people are saying."

"You should have just called the ranch." Sam softened his tone, but sat back with his arms crossed.

"Yeah, that's what he said." Georgia lowered her eyes.

"Who said?"

"Tyler. He said it the next morning, when I was taking him home."

"Huh."

Georgia lifted her chin, her neck growing splotchy, tears flowing harder in rebellion. Her voice shook as she spoke.

"But, look. I am a grown woman. I can make my own decisions about my life. What other people think of me is their problem, not mine. You don't have to defend me." She took a deep breath. "And Tyler's not as bad as everyone says he is." She wished she was a little bit like him, free to not care what anyone said. Or did he care?

Ellen took Georgia by the arms and guided her to their couch, sitting down with her. "Georgia, we love you. Sam has already punched Tyler's lights out once, you know."

Georgia had heard the story and had been extremely

RENA BELL YEAGER

embarrassed by it. Stories of the brawl, as it was being called, had been spread all over school. Sam and Tyler had punched each other until all the bags of mulch were busted, leaving wood chips all over the parking lot. Bloodied noses and black eyes were also included in the stories, and each time it was told, the story grew bigger. Some even said that Sam had a thing for her, and that they were fighting to see who got her. Never mind that Sam is happily married to her sister. The only true thing was the bloody nose. And that was one nose, not both. And it had been one punch, not two men mixing it up in the parking lot.

"Georgia?" Ellen drew her back to the conversation.

"Sam needs to stay out of it." She gave Sam her best teacher stare-down, making her point.

"How can I, when the people I am working with are talking about you?" Sam raised his hands in surrender. "I don't care about myself. But what people say about you affects Ellen, too. Did you know she has been stopped on the street with people offering advice on how to guide you?"

"Guide me? I'm not an errant teenager, and Ellen's not my mother. Those people are just a bunch of busy bodies." Georgia snapped, her green eyes on fire, eyebrows raised in punctuation. "You know what? I'm going home. People need to mind their own business, and that includes you, Sam." She grabbed her purse and walked out the door. But when she got to her car, she broke down and sobbed.

•—————••

REGGIE PUNCHED Tyler on the arm as he strolled into the bunkhouse. "You old snake. Finally made it with the teacher." Tyler cringed. For once, that phrase made him just a little sick.

He knew what Reggie was thinking. More than likely, so was the rest of the town by now.

Was that fair to Georgia? Was that what he wanted? He had originally intended just to have a couple of dates, a good time, maybe a kiss or two, or three, and then move on to the next woman. He hadn't planned to place any kind of brand on her. And he certainly hadn't set out to add her to his list of women, real or imagined, nor to make people think less of her.

"We didn't *make* anything. She actually rescued me, and now she is paying the price for it." He knew some of the gossips in town could be downright mean, but what they were doing to Georgia was criminal.

"Dude. I heard all about it from the bartender. He saw you on the dance floor, looking like you wanted to devour her. And when you left together, you were hanging all over her. Rumor has it you went back to her place. You telling me that isn't true?" Reggie looked Tyler in the eye.

"No. That part is true, I guess. I don't remember much of it, actually. And why are you getting so high and mighty? I seem to remember you leaving with some chick, too."

"Yeah." Reggie's eyes burned into Tyler's. "But she wasn't Georgia."

Tyler had to fix this. But what could he do that would dial back the talk? Whatever he did, it would be painful. He was certain of that.

# ELEVEN

GEORGIA SAT in her normal seat next to Ellen and Sam. Sam was still upset with her, but he was strong and supportive, sticking close to her, his hand on Ellen's back on one side, and his other hand on Georgia's shoulder as they entered the small sanctuary. His face was set in stone. Nobody dared to get close to them.

Still, she had felt and seen the stares. Some people nudged others while looking her way. Others turned away from her, ignoring her as she entered. She had never seen anyone treated this way in this church, especially by people she thought she knew and loved. It was enough to make her sick, and she was tempted to turn around and go home. Just in case she needed to throw up.

She listened to the music, but didn't feel like singing with it. No one in the congregation was perfect. She happened to know of plenty of folks who had hidden vices. The occasional look between two people across a room. The out-of-town flavor-of-the-day anonymous support groups. She had nothing against those kinds of groups. People needed support in many areas of their lives, and those groups did a good thing. But when people pointed at her, or snubbed her as a few had done this morning, she took exception to that. She picked up her Bible and pretended to follow the service. What was the preacher talking about, again? She opened the book to a random page and sighed.

Ellen wrapped her arm around Georgia's shoulders, almost as if she were holding her in place. At least, her sister was there for her. She resolved to stick to her seat on the end of the pew. It was on the aisle and would be easy to escape. But she sat firmly in her seat. She would not allow gossipers to chase her out.

•————————•

TYLER COULDN'T BELIEVE he was doing this. He normally didn't care what anybody thought of him. But here he was, driving into the church parking lot on Sunday morning. He found Georgia's little green car and parked his much larger diesel nearby. Hesitating, he finally opened the driver's side door. He could hear the music coming from the church and listened for just a moment. Then he stepped from the truck and closed the door as softly as possible behind him. The front doors of the hundred-year-old building were large, wooden, and imposing. Were they meant to keep out riff-raff like him? There was a sign on the door, but he didn't take time to look at it. He stopped at the back of the sanctuary to scan the congregation, and found Georgia sitting three rows from the front, next to Sam and Ellen, left side, on the center aisle.

He slipped into the back pew while they were singing. Belatedly, he took off his hat and ran his fingers through his hair, feeling the stares of the few people who had watched him enter. He was clean, had shaved, and was wearing his best shirt and jeans. He had even polished his boots and belt buckle. But he still felt dirty. Nevertheless, he was committed. He was going to do this. For her.

The sermon was something about a good Samaritan, but he was not really listening. In his mind he walked through what he was about to do. He sent up a quick prayer for courage, even though he never prayed. The preacher had met his eye when he walked in, so the man showed no surprise as Tyler left his seat during the final song and walked to the front of the church. Tyler shook the minister's hand then stood next to him with his hands clasped in front of him. He held his hat in his hands, and waited. Curious eyes watched him instead of looking at the words in their hymnals. He knew he was on display and worked hard to not fidget as he waited. Finally, the song ended and the preacher spoke.

"Ladies and gentlemen, please be seated," the pastor said to the congregation. It was the end of the service, and some of them had already picked up their purses and Bibles in order to make a quick exit. Tyler heard a couple of grumbles about missing lunch.

"This is Tyler Grant." The preacher motioned toward him. "Some of you may already know him, or know of him." The pastor cleared his throat to silence the murmuring, pausing to emphasize the last half of that statement.

"Tyler came to see me yesterday, at his request, to discuss some of the gossip that has been going around. Seems that some of it has been rather unflattering." The minister spoke clearly, enunciating each word so that there would be no doubt in what he had just said. "He asked to address the congregation, and I have given him my permission."

Tyler glanced briefly at Georgia, who sat wide-eyed and

frozen. She looked at Tyler with horror, one hand over her mouth, when Ellen reached over and took her other hand in support. Georgia closed her eyes before looking back at Tyler again. What was she thinking? Was he doing the right thing, or would he make matters worse?

He stood strong in front of the congregation. No wobbles today. He was stone-cold sober. He had made sure of that last night by staying back at the ranch and retiring early. Curious eyes across the room focused on him as he cleared his throat. *Here goes nothing.*

"I came here today to talk about something that occurred last week. I've already talked to the preacher, and he knows what I'm going to say." Tyler scanned the room as several people fidgeted in their seats. He returned his eyes forward, away from Georgia.

"Last week, a beautiful lady rescued me when I was drunk and stupid. Since then, there have been a lot of rumors going around about what happened. People who weren't there decided for themselves what we did or didn't do, and even shared those ideas with others on social media, at their jobs, and here at church." Tyler moved his hat from one hand to the other. The pastor placed his hand on Tyler's shoulder in support and patted him before pulling it away again.

"So let me tell you what did happen." An older couple in the second row whispered to each other. Tyler ignored them. He glanced briefly at Georgia, who was focusing on her hands in her lap, then turned his eyes to the congregation again.

"This beautiful lady took me to her home and gave me a safe place to sleep it off. On her couch. The next morning, she fed me and took me back to the ranch. On the way, she sang to me. Yes. She sang to me. It was a song about a garden, about love and fidelity, and gave me a little bit of hope for myself."

Several people looked at each other as if in disbelief. But

Georgia had been scheduled to sing that morning, and they all knew that. So this detail should not have been a surprise to anyone. Tyler shuffled slightly, then continued.

"Some of you look doubtful. I see a few snickers, too, and rolling eyes. But I don't know what's wrong with what she did. She was compassionate, but she was also stern. She put me in my place, like the teacher she is. I bet all her students toe the line, but I bet they also love her."

"I don't know what I'm saying here, but I felt like I needed to say something."

The room was getting warm. He focused his gaze over the pews as a hundred pair of eyes waited, and took a deep breath.

"Look. I'm just a poor, desperate cowboy, trying to be something that I'm not. Trying to be worth something that I'm not." He crunched his hat brim in his fist. "And I'm probably guilty of most of the things you have said about me at one time or another, and deserve your gossip. But she . . . this beautiful lady . . . doesn't."

Tyler turned to Georgia one more time, his gray eyes sad. She looked so lovely. Hair down around her shoulders today, pink blouse perfectly crisp without a single wrinkle, green eyes now lifted to his and watching him in wonder. He closed his own eyes for just a moment, then looked straight at her with a wry smile.

"Please forgive me, Georgia. I'm thankful for your kindness. You deserve better than what you have received in return. And I hope this helps to set the record straight, and stop the rumors." He paused, just the barest of heartbeats, as if he was going to say more. Then he turned his focus back to the center aisle and walked out the door.

His heart was catawampus. Somewhere in the middle of trying to make amends, his emotions had nearly gotten the better of him, sending his brain spinning. He shook himself after walking through the paneled double doors where the sign on the outside said "Welcome," and stuck his hat on his head, trying to put his heart back in order. He hadn't felt welcomed at all.

He had no intention of, well, really, he didn't know what his intentions were. All he knew was that he was confused, and he didn't know how that had happened. He always held himself in check, even when he was in hot pursuit of the next pretty girl. He had never allowed his heart to become involved. Until now.

Outside, Tyler opened the door to his truck. It had been a long time since he had felt love for anybody, but his heart pulled toward Georgia in a way he had never felt before. How he wished things could be different. He slid behind the steering wheel, watching some of the people who had heard his explanation as they crossed the parking lot to their cars. A few looked at him, then looked away. He didn't know if that was because of shame, or guilt, or if they were shunning him. It didn't matter, really. These were her people, not his. He would never fit in.

• •———————• •

"THANK you for what you did last Sunday."

It was several days before Georgia had gotten up the nerve to send the text, needing time to process everything. She had been stunned and sat there in shocked silence while Tyler walked out the door, taking her heart with him. The problem was, he didn't know it, and she couldn't tell him. She was Georgia Duncan. Teacher. Girl Next Door. Sang in the church choir. Never got into any kind of trouble from the time she was a child. They would never fit. But oh, how she wanted to try.

A few people apologized to her after the service, but there were still a lot of wary glances, as if they weren't sure what to think of this new development. Her thoughts returned to her phone as three dots floated.

"I had to do something for you. I can't believe how vicious some people can be."

"It was very gallant of you." Georgia still couldn't believe Tyler had stood up for her in front of the whole church.

"I'm no hero. If I hadn't gotten drunk, the whole thing wouldn't have happened."

"Well, I still appreciate what you did."

Crickets. Georgia waited, but Tyler didn't respond. There weren't even any floating dots. Maybe she had interrupted him while he was in the middle of doing something. Work? Or something else? It was six p.m. She didn't know when his work day wrapped up, or if it ever did. Maybe he didn't have anything else to say. Not giving up, she sent another message.

"You're not a poor, desperate cowboy. You remember that song we heard at the fair? You should listen to it again."

"Which song?" That response came back fast.

"Desperado."

More crickets. He wasn't responding. She tapped her fingers on the dining table as she thought about her next words.

"Can we get together for another picnic by the lake at the ranch? I'll bring the sandwiches this time."

"Why?"

The one-word question came back way too quickly. Georgia took a full five minutes of her own to respond. Did he not want to meet again? Maybe he just wanted to put it all behind him. She finally took a breath and dove in.

"I just want to set the record straight. About you. You know, since you set the record straight about me to everyone at church."

Although she wasn't sure it helped all that much. She still heard whispers in the hallway at school.

Why was she pushing this? She should just leave well enough alone. She remembered her dad using that phrase a few times when she or Ellen continued to bother him about something they wanted, or wanted to do. Was she doing that to Tyler?

•┄┄┄┄┄┄•

TYLER SAW the text pop up on his phone and thought back to those few days ago when he apologized for his behavior to her church congregation. He hoped she might follow him out of the church that day, but had then seen the shock on her face and realized that was too much to ask. So why was she reaching out to him now? Maybe he should just end it here.

He squinched his eyes together against the sun as he read the last message. His fingers hovered over his phone as he debated.

"Something wrong?" Reggie watched as Tyler read and responded to the messages. They had been working the fences again. Seemed they were always in need of repair.

"Nothing wrong. You got that string of wire tightened?" He wasn't going to discuss this with anybody. Not even Reggie.

A few days later, he was sitting in his truck, thinking. He connected his phone to the speakers and surfed for "Desperado" on the internet. Finding it, he listened to it again, wondering what Georgia had been talking about. Yeah, yeah, yeah. He was riding fences with his life, he knew that. He literally rode fence lines all day long. Then living life hard at night, ignoring the urging in his soul, but still wanting it. And wanting it bad.

The final words of the song made him sit up straight. Let somebody love him? What was she trying to say? Was she that somebody? Was it too late? Or was it not too late?

Maybe there was hope after all. She wanted another picnic. Maybe this was another chance.

# TWELVE

TYLER TIGHTENED the straps holding down the six rolls of barbed wire he had just purchased from the Farm and Ranch Store. He hated barbed wire. It was too easy for animals to get tangled in it and when they did, they could be severely injured. Barbed wire cut into the flesh, especially around the legs where the muscles had less protection. Barbed wire left scars. Deep lasting scars. And sometimes an animal had to be put down if the wound was too deep.

Seeing Georgia that day at her church had hurt, and he had seen the hurt on her face too. The rumors that had circulated tangled around them, cutting deeply. Normally he was not bothered by such things, and he had never been concerned about the impact his actions had on others. But the pain in Georgia's eyes was more than he could bear. He had strung her along, just as assuredly as he was going to string this barbed wire.

Tyler drove toward the ranch, "Desperado" blaring on his radio. After much thought, he had finally agreed to the picnic, and she was coming out later today.

The two-lane farm road was paved, but narrow. A beat-up Toyota sedan with a different color hood and front quarter panel sped around him from behind. It swerved to miss an armadillo that was in the middle of the road and lost control, spinning into the path of Tyler's truck. Tyler tried to miss the Toyota as it spun, but he slid in the gravel shoulder and lost traction, landing upside down in the deep gully that ran alongside the road. His body crunched in pain. The Toyota sped out of sight.

The steering wheel was bent where he had pushed against it. The airbag had deployed with the impact and deflated immediately, sending a cloud of dust that had him coughing. He was mostly upside down, having been thrown against the driver's side door, even with the seatbelt cinched tightly.

His phone was in his back pocket, but he couldn't get to it. He started pushing buttons on his steering wheel, praying that the Bluetooth would connect and allow him to call 911. Instead, he hit the channel up button and somehow connected to a radio station playing gospel music. He heard a country singer crooning the song that Georgia had sung to him about a garden, and love, and fidelity. The final chorus echoed in his head, over and over, as everything went black.

•—————•

GEORGIA WAS DRIVING along the farm road toward the ranch and saw what looked like truck wheels sticking up out of a deep ditch. No other cars were around, and heat waves radiated from the chassis. She pulled over to the side of the road, just beyond the wreck where there was a slim shoulder, and ran to the dry creek bed. It was a good thing there was no water in it this time of year. If there had been, whoever was in the truck might have drowned.

Her fingers shook as she pulled her phone out of her pocket and dialed 911, staying on the phone until they had the location from her GPS. She dialed Tyler's number next and received his voicemail. Three more tries had the same result. What should she do now? What should she do?

She paced along the road, hoping the emergency responders would arrive quickly. Thinking again, she tapped her phone and called Sam.

Sam was first on the scene. She couldn't tell from the way the truck was laying in the ditch if it was Tyler's or not, but her gut told her it was. Sam looked for a way to pry the passenger door open but it was too mangled. And with the truck face down he couldn't get to the windshield or the back window. Several rolls of barbed wire also blocked his access. But then he found a hat lying in the ditch, caught in a cluster of thorny brambles. He picked it up and dusted it off before handing it to Georgia, his face grim.

"It's Tyler's." Georgia's voice was flat. She crossed her arms over her chest and looked away, trying not to cry.

"Yeah. I thought so. I tried to get in, but the cab is blocked on all sides. Let's hope he's not in too bad of a shape."

It seemed like an hour of waiting, but it was actually only a few minutes before the police and fire department arrived. First responders dressed in their heavy turnout gear and protective helmets began cutting the vehicle apart, stabilizing it with large airbags before using their heavy powered tools to remove the doors and the windshield. Then they confirmed her worst fear.

Tyler was unconscious and bleeding. She swiped a tear away, not willing to think the worst just yet. But still, the fear sat there on the edge of her heart. Would he live? God wasn't done with him yet, was He?

An air ambulance was staged in an open field not far from the accident. Sam held Georgia close while Tyler's body was slowly pulled from the wreckage, a two-piece backboard snapped behind and on either side of his body. Sandbags were strapped around his head, a cervical collar on his neck. Officers said he would be taken to University Hospital in San Antonio, which was the Level One trauma center closest to their town. At least he was alive. But just barely. Georgia stared without seeing, hugging herself as the helicopter rose slowly from the ground. Tears flowed freely now, and she didn't even bother to try to contain them as she watched the aircraft disappear into the sun.

"Sam? Will you take me to the hospital? I need to be there for him. Please." Georgia couldn't stop her voice from shaking.

His hug was warm. "Sure. Let's get your car to my house, and I'll follow you. Are you okay to drive a few miles?"

Georgia nodded, but she felt numb.

"Okay. If you are sure. I'll be right behind you. I'll also call Randall Hudson to let him know what is going on."

The ninety-minute drive took nearly two hours when they got stuck behind a convoy of farm trucks taking a harvest of cotton to the processor. Georgia tapped her foot nervously the entire way, wringing her hands and trying not to cry any more than she already had. She needed to be strong for Tyler.

Ellen called to say she activated the prayer chain at church, and the minister called for a special service to pray for Tyler. She said they prayed for his healing, but they also prayed for forgiveness for the way they had treated him and Georgia. Georgia hoped they weren't too late. Tyler needed to know that he was loved by people. And by God.

GEORGIA AND SAM sat in the waiting room, Sam flipping through a magazine, obviously not reading or seeing what was in it. She swung one crossed leg to the beat of the music that played softly from the overhead speakers, oblivious to the song. Muted beeps and voices could be heard from behind the double doors. One hour turned into three before a doctor finally approached them.

"Are you Tyler's family?"

"He doesn't have any family. I'm his girlfriend." Sam looked at her sideways. It was a small fib.

"His injuries are severe, and we need to do surgery immediately, to repair some internal damage. We need someone to sign for him."

The sliding doors opened and closed as Mr. Hudson entered the waiting room. Thank God he was there. They explained the situation to him and he quickly signed. He didn't question Georgia's presence. They simply huddled together and said a quick prayer for Tyler. He was in God's hands, now.

· · —————— · ·

FOUR HOURS LATER, Tyler was out of recovery and in a private room. Georgia tapped on the door before pushing it open to peek in.

"Hey."

Tyler grunted in response. He was droopy-eyed from the pain medication, but he still tracked Georgia with his gray spheres as she entered the room. She kept her face stoic as she scanned his injuries. The left side of his face was bruised where he had hit the window as the truck rolled. His left eye was also black, and he had a broken nose where the airbag had thrown his arm into his face. They hadn't fixed that yet.

The IV in his right arm was connected to three different bags. His left shoulder was immobilized in plaster that went down his arm to his fingers, that arm bent over his chest. It was also held by a sling that was wrapped around his torso. She couldn't see any other injuries since he was covered with the sheet and blankets, but she knew there were more.

Several wires ran from under the sheets where they were attached to his chest, leading to the monitor that was located on the other side of the bed. A blood pressure cuff was wrapped around his good arm. Georgia heard the click and buzz as it filled up then slowly deflated, and she read the numbers on the monitor. One twenty over eighty. Normal. Respirations twenty. Pulse eighty-two. Not too bad all things considered. She touched his good arm as she sat in the chair beside his bed. His pulse increased.

"The doctor said you have several broken bones, including your nose and a couple of cracked ribs, but your shoulder and leg are the worst, along with some internal damage. I guess you were crunched up pretty badly." She swallowed. "Sam and Mr. Hudson are out in the waiting room. I know you don't have any other family."

"Don' worry 'bout me. I've had broken bones before." Tyler tried to laugh but coughed instead. His words were fuzzy and slurred.

"These are not simple fractures," she indicated toward his shoulder and leg. "You will need rehab. It may take several weeks."

"Why're you here?" The question made her pull her hand back from his arm. Did he not want her here?

"You don't remember, do you?"

"What should I be 'membering?" The puzzled expression on his face told her he was genuinely confused.

"We were going to have another picnic. I was on my way to

the ranch when I found your truck upside down in the ditch that runs along the farm road."

"Bob-wire."

"Yeah. There were several rolls of barbed wire that made it hard for the firemen to get to you."

"You called f'r help?" The monitor beeped as his pulse and blood pressure spiked.

"Yes, I called 911, and then Sam. And I watched while they pulled you out of the truck. I was so afraid that . . ."

The nurse entered, interrupting their conversation. Georgia stood back as the woman took his blood pressure again, using an old-fashioned cuff.

"I'm sorry, ma'am. I'm going to have to ask you to leave. You can come back tomorrow, after Mr. Grant has had a chance to get some rest." Her stern expression suggested Georgia's presence might have been the cause of the change in his vitals.

"I'll come back tomorrow afternoon. I'm really sorry about all of this." She swept her hand through the air, indicating his injuries. She wanted to squeeze his hand, but the nurse stood between them.

"Iss okay. Wasn' your fault. I was on ranch biznes."

Georgia nodded and left.

THE NEXT FEW days went by in a blur. Tyler's leg and his shoulder were both reconstructed with pins and rods. He was going to be one of those men who always knew when the weather was going to change because he could "feel it in his bones." He chuckled to himself at the thought and hoped he wouldn't ache too badly. He was afraid it would make him feel old. But truthfully, he was happy to be alive.

His injuries had been due to the force of the accident, starting with his driving leg, which he had slammed against the brake, up through his seatbelt across his chest and shoulder, which had tightened up on impact to hold him in his seat. He had bruises across his pelvis and chest, and now stitches from the surgeries to repair a rip in his spleen. The doctor said it was a miracle that he survived.

He hoped he would be able to go back to his job as a ranch hand—as long as he followed instructions and took his rehab seriously. But it would take several weeks. The doctor implied with a look over his reading glasses that he thought Tyler might not follow the rules. Yeah, that was Tyler all right, right down to his very core. But successful recovery was dependent on him obeying, so he would play nice.

The nurses told him Georgia had visited him a couple of times but he had slept through both of those visits. He missed being able to see her, but it was probably better this way.

•——————•

"I BROUGHT YOUR HAT." She was back. Tyler sighed as Georgia entered the hospital room. He was being discharged and sent to a rehab facility for a couple of weeks.

"I thought it was lost. Where did you find it?" Tyler had already mourned his hat, thinking it was destroyed in the accident. But he was glad to see it in Georgia's hands. The hat held special meaning to him, even if it was beat-up.

"Sam found it in the ditch. I guess it flew out the window when the truck rolled. It was pretty dirty, so I cleaned it up for you." She handed it to Tyler and he flipped it over in his hand, noticing it had a few more scars.

"How long do they expect you to be in rehab?" It was small talk, but better than silence.

"The doctor is saying several weeks. Part of it inpatient, and most of it outpatient. I'm not quite sure how that is going to work yet, or where I'm going for outpatient."

"I'm sure it will work out. Is it okay if I come to see you at the inpatient facility?"

Tyler gazed at Georgia. "Are you sure you want to?"

"Yes, Tyler. You will need visitors to break up the monotony."

"They will keep me busy, and I'll probably be tired, sore, and grumpy from all the work they will make me do."

"Then I'll bring cookies."

Her green eyes sparkled with something. Mischief? Why was she being so nice to him? He decided to accept her offer for what it was.

"Okay then. I'll make sure your name is on the visitor's list."

"Thanks. Well, I'll see you there then, in a couple of days." She turned to leave, running her finger along the foot of the bed as she did.

"Yeah. See ya then." Tyler wasn't quite sure what to think. But he did know one thing. His life had definitely changed as a result of the accident. And he had no idea where he was going from here.

# THIRTEEN

GEORGIA, Sam, and Mr. Hudson were all visiting Tyler in the rehab facility. He had spent four days in the hospital and was transferred to the inpatient center from there, staying another week. Georgia visited him every day after school.

They were gathered around him while the doctor was discussing his outpatient options. He couldn't be alone since he would need help with basic things like hygiene and dressing. He would have a visiting nurse for that. And he would have in-home visits by a physical therapist. But he would also need help with food, laundry, and general living.

"He can stay with me." Georgia's words startled everyone. She had thought about it for a while, but had not mentioned it to anyone.

"No!" Sam, Mr. Hudson, and Tyler all spoke at the same time.

"Why not?" She looked at each of them, hands on her hips. "I have a spare bedroom, I'm on the ground floor, and there will be plenty of room for the wheelchair. I'll be at school during the day, so the visiting nurse and physical therapists can make their visits while I'm gone. In the evening I'll be there and can fix supper for him. It'll just be for a couple of weeks, right?"

The doctor cleared his throat. "It will probably be closer to four or six weeks."

Mr. Hudson spoke up. "He can stay in one of the ground floor rooms in our guest house. He will have a cook and room service available. Our ranch insurance is covering everything."

Sam agreed. "That makes the most sense." Georgia knew he would object. He did not want Tyler to stay with her. That would break every rule in Sam's brother-in-law handbook.

"Please. I want to help." She turned to Tyler. "I feel partly responsible for all of this. I have the room. My place is in town, much closer to the hospital and doctor's office. And the therapists won't have to drive fifteen miles outside of town every day."

They all started talking at the same time until Tyler spoke up.

"Wait." He pointed to his chest. "I'm the patient. It is my decision, isn't it? Unless some kind of worker's comp rules say I have to stay on the ranch?"

"No. There are no rules like that." Mr. Hudson nodded his head, his brows furrowed.

The doctor looked between them all, watching the conversation. Georgia wondered what he was thinking. But he stayed silent. This wasn't his decision. And it wasn't hers, either.

Tyler studied Georgia's face, then looked around at the others. Four sets of eyes waited for his answer. He paused, then held out his good hand to her, touching only her fingers.

"Look, I appreciate everyone's concern. But Georgia is right. Her place is the closest one to the therapists and the hospital in case something goes wrong. Not that it will." He lifted his hand as a stop sign as they all started to speak again. "We'll try it for a week or so. If it gets too uncomfortable for you, Georgia, just say the word and I will go to the ranch."

Tyler turned toward Sam, holding out his good arm for a handshake. "I promise not to touch her. You have my word."

"You know the gossip mill will love this." Sam squeezed his lips into a flat line.

"They'll find somebody else to talk about before long." Georgia was determined.

Sam looked at the ceiling and sighed. She wondered if he was getting tired of fighting. Then he lowered his gaze, his face fierce, staring long and hard at Tyler, who didn't flinch.

"Okay. Let's get you settled, then."

* * *

SAM AND ELLEN helped Tyler settle into Georgia's apartment. They weren't happy with the decision, but she insisted, since Tyler had no family to help. It was all one floor, had plenty of room to move around, and would give Tyler the privacy he needed as he did his therapy while she was at school. Georgia had also pointed out that she had a spare bedroom, and nothing inappropriate was going to happen. How could it, when he was trussed up like a Thanksgiving turkey on half his body?

A therapist and visiting nurse were scheduled to visit through the week. They would assist Tyler with his physical therapy and personal needs.

The church set up a meal train that would provide meals for Georgia and Tyler Monday through Friday. They would eat leftovers or whatever she prepared on the weekend. That would relieve her from working all day, grading assignments in the evening, and still having to cook for the two of them.

Tyler sat in his wheelchair, looking around at the reasonably large apartment. He would never have guessed its size from the outside. Of course, he had been here the night he was drunk, but hadn't taken the time to really see Georgia's home.

Her front wall held a large picture window. The single pane measured about four feet wide, if he guessed correctly. Two side panes opened by sliding up. Another six feet to the side was her front door, which had a peephole to the outside.

The back wall of the living area held her couch. He remembered thinking it was surprisingly comfortable, with its micro-soft fabric. Nothing fancy. Just plain brown, with three cushions. Two side tables flanked the couch, and an ottoman of the same fabric sat in front of it. It would be easy enough to get from his wheelchair to the couch. A single cushioned armchair in the same style sat against the wall to the right, and the room opened to the dining table and kitchen to the left.

Sam and Ellen left, and Tyler felt suddenly strange. Now what? He decided to break the ice with a nickname.

"Hey, Shortcake. Why do you live in an apartment between two busy bodies? I would picture you living in a trendier part of town." He remembered seeing curtains flutter each time he had brought Georgia home. Might as well tease her since he would be here for a while.

Georgia tilted her head, as if considering her answer. She was scratching the cat he learned was named Lily behind the ears. "Shortcake? Then I guess you're Crip." She shot him a grin. "It's convenient and affordable. My neighbors are nice and quiet, even if they are nosy. And I did have a roommate for about a year. After she left, I decided I liked the extra space, so I kept the place." She focused on him and smiled, showing her dimple. "Why do you live in a bunkhouse filled with smelly men?" The smile transformed into a smirk.

"It's convenient and affordable. And although it can get smelly," Tyler pinched his nose to demonstrate, "they are a good bunch of guys."

"How did you know where I live? When you picked me up for that first date?" She sat in the single chair with the cat on her lap.

Tyler shrugged, then cringed. Shrugging was hard with one shoulder bound up in plaster. "All the guys at the ranch know where you live. I think most of them are sweet on you."

"Them?" Georgia's eyes twinkled as she leaned back in the chair.

He tried to get more comfortable. "You're cute. Even a smelly ranch hand can like cute."

That made Georgia laugh. He liked seeing the dimple in her left cheek pop out.

"Do you need a pillow? Or maybe some help with moving to the couch? You can put your leg up on the ottoman." Georgia leaned forward and put the cat down. She moved the wheelchair in front of the couch, sideways, and helped him slide from one to the other. He grunted in pain.

"A pillow for my arm would be good. And maybe elevating my leg would help."

Georgia left the room and returned a minute later with two fluffy pillows. "I got these from my bed. They should help."

"I don't want to take your pillows. What are you going to sleep with?" He widened his eyes.

"I have plenty." Oh. Of course. Didn't most women have lots of pillows? At least, that's what he had heard. He felt weird letting her stuff the pillows around him, but it did make him more comfortable.

They ordered from a meal delivery service for their first

night, getting spaghetti and salad from a local restaurant. It was not very easy to twist the noodles with one hand, but he managed. The meals came in disposable dishes, which made clean-up easy, and Georgia told him to relax while she cleaned. He felt like he should be helping, but then again, he was here because he couldn't do those simple things.

Later that night, Tyler studied the spare bedroom, looking for hints of Georgia's personality. An antique four-poster bed took up half the room, with a dresser on the opposite wall and a desk in front of the window, which faced the parking lot in the front. His beat-up black hat hung on the post at the end of the bed, nearest the door. She must have put it there.

A beautiful handmade quilt covered the bed. He remembered Georgia's fascination with the quilts when they had gone to the fair together. This quilt was in a crazy, haphazard pattern, the colors brown and blue instead of the frilly, girly pinks he expected. The curtain was in similar colors. Was this room always decorated like this, or had she done it for him? He shook his head. Georgia was like a jigsaw puzzle. Maybe being here would give him a chance to put together some of the pieces.

Lily entered the room like she owned it, tail high in the air, giving him the evil eye. She jumped on the bed and curled up on one of his pillows. Tyler did not like cats. He swatted her away, closing his door behind her. She meowed loudly as she left, obviously upset that her domain had been invaded.

• •————————• •

TYLER SPENT the first few days of his confinement at Georgia's apartment watching videos on his phone. People came up with crazy things to put on the Internet. Didn't they know their stupid stunts were dangerous? And how did they get paid for these things? Did they have a real job? He shook his head. He was starting to sound like his father.

He didn't want to think of his time here as confinement, but that was essentially what it was. With very limited mobility he was dependent on others for most everything. He hoped it wouldn't be too stifling for either of them. Hygiene, therapy, videos, and watching Georgia in the evening as he sat on her couch was his routine. He didn't want to cramp her space, and he knew he would go stir-crazy before long.

He turned to watch her again as she sat at her dining table grading assignments from her laptop. It was a nightly occurrence. He remembered the written assignments from his middle school days, and the red pencils that his teachers used when grading them. But now most student assignments were electronic, and Georgia was working from her computer.

"You're staring." She looked up from her keyboard. She must have keen teacher senses.

"You're easy to stare at, Shortcake." Tyler refused to look away. Georgia blinked first. He tilted his head. "Does this make you uncomfortable, me being here?"

"No, we've already had this conversation. You need a place to stay while you recover. And I've got room. I'm at school most of the day and we are only here together a couple of hours in the evening. It should be okay. Right?" She was clearly in teacher mode.

"Why are you doing this for me?" He spoke quietly, and waited for her answer.

Georgia looked down, pink splotching up her neck in embarrassment. "I just think it is something God wants me to do."

Tyler scoffed. "Why would God care about me?" He hoped she wouldn't try to preach a sermon every night. If so, he would have to go back to the ranch. He was not a religious guy.

Georgia turned back to him and searched his eyes. "God cares about all of us, Tyler. Even when we don't care about Him."

He looked away and changed the subject. "How long have you been teaching school?"

Her face brightened like a ray of sunshine. She obviously liked her job. "I've been at Nora Hills since graduating with my master's degree in Education. About six years now. And I love my job. I teach math and science."

Was it as challenging to corral a herd of eighth graders as he thought it might be? He would rather herd cattle. A quick mental calculation told him she was about thirty years old, to his thirty-three.

"I am amazed at the patience you have with your students."

"They're curious adolescents. You know, they ask nearly every day how you are doing. They had been giving me a bit of trouble when you and I first started doing things together, but now they want to know more about you. I think they are intrigued with the mystery called Tyler Grant. You do have a bit of a reputation, you know." She continued clicking on her laptop, occasionally squinting her eyes or laughing at an answer.

"What's fun about teaching?" He was sincerely interested.

"I have always liked working with my students. They are at a difficult age, and my prayer is that I can help give them a sense of balance that they may not get anywhere else. If I can do that, along with teaching them math and science, I will have accomplished my goal as a teacher."

"What kind of math are you teaching in the eighth grade?"

Georgia raised her head, looking at him squarely in the

face. "We're in algebra and some geometry. Why do you ask, Crip?" She wiggled her eyebrows.

Tyler shrugged, but had a new sparkle in his eyes. "No particular reason. I play math games from time to time. Numbers have always interested me."

"Hm. Can you show me some of what you do with numbers to entertain yourself? The more I can make a subject entertaining and interesting for my students, the more they might actually study."

Georgia rose from the table and sat beside him on the couch, placing her laptop in front of him and leaning over his shoulder. Tyler breathed in. Honeysuckle. Yeah, he remembered going home after that disastrous night spent watching the moon, and smelling her sweet scent for a week. Even after a shower. The nose has a memory, and it had stuck with him. He applied his attention to the laptop and slid the fingers of his good hand over the glide pad while struggling to stay composed.

He showed her some of the sites he liked to visit where he could play math or number games against other users, and how she could create profiles to allow her students to play against each other. When she leaned in closer, he wondered if she knew what she was doing to him. But this was Georgia. Wholesome. Pure. There was nothing coy about the way she was leaning toward him now. No agenda like most of the women he knew. He breathed in deeply and let it out slowly, hoping she wouldn't notice her effect on him.

She jumped from the couch and rose to stand in front of him, excited. "Would you be willing to share some of your tips and tricks with my class? I can set up an electronic meeting where we can share screens in real-time, and arrange for a laptop from the school for you to use. Would you do that for them?" She put her hands together in a prayer pose, pleading.

He was humbled. Of course, he would do it. It would help pass the day, and if it would help her students, then all the better. But first, he needed a bucket of ice water thrown in his face. The room had gotten warm.

••————————••

TWO DAYS later Georgia started the web meeting and introduced Tyler to her students.

She had tried to ignore the buzz in her brain as she leaned over Tyler that day. All man. There was something unique about him that she couldn't put her finger on. Maybe it was his scent. Soap, saddle, and sunshine. With a little bit of horse. She shook her head to focus.

Tyler drew genuine interest as he interacted with the kids, showing them some of his favorite tricks for quick mental calculations, and some of his favorite online games, both solo and multi-user. He was a natural with them, and she watched in amazement as the students, quiet at first, got into the spirit of the lesson. He was like a Pied Piper, anticipating their questions and answering them with ease. Her heart fluttered as he challenged them to think of the myriad of ways they would use numbers throughout their lives. She blinked when she heard him ask if she wanted to wrap up the session. The lesson had flown by.

"Okay. Time for final questions for Tyler. Anyone?" There were just a few minutes left in the online session.

Emily's hand shot up first. "Are you the teacher's pet?" The classroom erupted in snickers.

Georgia blushed as Tyler's image on the big screen laughed, but she gave the thirteen-year-old her sternest look.

"Emily. That was totally inappropriate. Let's keep the questions about math, okay? Next question."

"It's alright, Georgia. I'll answer her." He had been wearing the black hat throughout the session, and now he took it off and got closer to the camera. His gray eyes sparkled with mischief. "It's Emily, right?" The girl nodded.

"I respect Miss Duncan immensely. But I'll tell you a secret about her if you promise not to tell anyone." He looked back and forth with the pair of grays as if to check if others were listening. They all grew quiet. He definitely had their attention, and she wondered what he was going to say, hoping he didn't embarrass her.

"Miss Duncan works after school every day, and sometimes after dark," he held his finger to his lips to emphasize the secret, "grading your homework and tests, and making sure that each of you are learning the things she is trying to teach you, instead of just giving you a free pass." Now he backed up just a little. "You are all going to be in high school next year. She wants you to be prepared. So, really, you are all the teacher's pet. Every single one of you."

The kids were silent. They hadn't thought of Georgia that way. And she gained a new respect for Tyler, as well. But her heart pounded in her chest as she saw his rugged but handsome face in a new light. Maybe some of the rumors about him were wrong.

⁕——————⁕

THE MEAL TRAIN set up by the church was working pretty well. Most of the ladies who were providing food were bringing it to the apartment in the late afternoon, after Georgia was home from work. The older ladies were nice enough, if a bit snoopy. They would say hello, ask him how he was doing, and if there was anything else they could do for him. Then they would talk to Georgia for a while and leave after a few minutes. They would also look around the apartment, their eyes wandering as they visited. What they were looking for, he didn't know. Some would openly stare at him, as if he were some kind of prize. He knew they were trying to assess the relationship between him and Georgia. He could handle that, too, especially if they were being protective of her. But it was the visits from the single women that made him uneasy.

One day, it was early afternoon. Georgia was still at school, and the therapists had been gone for about an hour when there was a knock on the door. Two young ladies stood there, looking like they were barely of adult age. They each held a covered dish, so Tyler thanked them and asked them to set the dishes on the dining table. Unfortunately, now they were both in the apartment with him. Alone. He stuck out his hand. "I'm Tyler. Thanks again for the food."

"I'm Sarah."

"And I'm Sayla."

"And we're sisters." They talked in tandem. And giggled.

Tyler scowled. They were both blonde and beautiful. He might have even seen them together at the Blue Bull a time or two. He wasn't quite sure. But he knew the look in their eyes and what they were thinking as they looked at each other and then back at him. They giggled again.

*Nip this in the bud quick, Tyler. These girls are trouble.* He talked low to himself, then lifted his voice to them.

"It's nice to meet you ladies, but I'm afraid I don't have time to visit. My therapist is coming in just a few minutes. But thank you again for the food." It was a small lie, but the first thing he could think of. These girls were from the church. They were doing a big favor by providing a home-cooked meal. But they looked at him like he was a piece of meat.

"We could stick around. Keep you company until he comes." They almost pleaded with their eyes.

But Tyler had played this game in his rowdy days. And before he met Georgia, he wouldn't have minded the distraction. Now he had no desire to get tangled up in a situation that would surely lead to trouble for everyone involved.

"I'm sorry ladies. But I think you should go home to your mama." It was a harsh statement, his tone as sharp as his words, but it made his point.

The disappointment was plainly visible on each of the girls' faces. He would have no proof if they decided to stretch the truth about the visit. But they finally left, and he let out a breath as he closed the door behind them with his good foot.

When Georgia came home from school, she saw the casseroles sitting on the table. "They came by already? Who was it today? I thought Mrs. Engleman wasn't coming until later."

"It was two girls. Sisters. Sarah and somebody. I don't remember the other name."

"Mrs. Engleman sent her daughters?" Georgia widened her eyes in surprise. "Mrs. Engleman is one of those... oh, I don't know... people who judges everyone. Except her daughters, if you get my meaning."

"Yeah, I was not comfortable with them being here and got them out the door as quickly as I could. But don't be surprised if you hear more gossip."

Georgia frowned.

"Nothing happened, but the way they looked at me gave me the shivers." Tyler shook his head and one good shoulder.

"You know you don't have to answer the door. They can leave the dishes outside. In fact, I'll put a small table out there with a box on it for the food, and let the meal train know to only bring stuff by after four o'clock. When I'm home."

"Don't make a fuss over it..."

"It's not a fuss." She cut him off. "It's for your protection. And mine, actually. We don't need any more rumors than we already have floating around."

He nodded, then looked her in the eye. "You sure about this?"

"It'll be fine, Tyler." But his question had her wondering the same thing. What were they doing?

# FOURTEEN

BY THE FOLLOWING FRIDAY, Tyler had reached his limit of boredom. Therapy only went so far in passing the day. There was usually still a couple of hours between the time the therapist left and Georgia returned home from work. Mr. Hudson had come by one day to visit. Since he was on ranch business at the time of the accident, their workman's comp insurance was taking care of the bills. He promised Tyler he would still have a job when he was ready to come back.

Lily jumped onto his lap. On reflex, he swiped his arm to knock the cat off onto the floor. She looked at him as if he had struck her, which, of course, he had done, then she jumped onto her perch to continue staring back at him. It was a little unnerving—being stuck inside with an animal that he didn't like. But it made him feel a bit guilty, too. After all, he was the one who had invaded her space.

Glancing around and feeling a little like he was snooping, Tyler looked for pictures. There were none on the walls. Maybe that was an apartment rule or something. But there was a small upright piano, like the one in his grandmother's family room, that Georgia had moved toward the wall next to the neighboring apartment so that Tyler could navigate his wheelchair to the dining table. Pictures of her and her sister sat on top, and he got closer, but he couldn't reach them. One was of a younger Georgia and Ellen, heads tilted together. He smiled at the mischief in their eyes.

Tyler wondered about Georgia's love of music. He had not heard her play, but she obviously liked to sing. What was her background? Had she studied music in college? Or did it just come naturally? He knew there were people who couldn't read a single note, yet could play a plethora of instruments. Did Georgia have that kind of talent?

He used his uninjured arm to push the wheel of his chair, and his left foot for additional leverage, and wedged himself beside the table, next to the piano. Lifting the lid over the keyboard, he ran his fingers across the ivory keys. It was a beautiful instrument, fitting for a woman like Georgia. He plinked the keys out of boredom, not paying much attention to the notes, which rang clearly and in perfect tune.

*"Twinkle, twinkle little star*
*How I wonder what you are."*

It reminded him of the night they had fallen asleep under the pink moon. Which led to Sam slugging him.

Shutting the lid, he scooted back to the couch to watch more videos, this time watching a man cook over an open fire using eighteenth-century tools and recipes. He needed to find something to do.

Later that evening, Tyler watched as Georgia graded more assignments. He cleared his throat, drawing her attention away from the laptop. Nodding to the piano, he asked simply, "Do you play?"

Georgia looked over at the piano and back at Tyler with a smirk. "How about you scoot over here and let's find out?"

Georgia slid the dining table against the opposite wall to make room for the wheelchair. She sat down at the bench and raised the lid. Then she raised her arms like Beethoven, fingers dangling over the keys.

Tyler leaned in to watch. She didn't have any music in front of her. Georgia started with a small tune, one he didn't recognize. Smiling with one brow quirked up, her eyes twinkling at him, she scooted away from him on the bench and patted the empty space. "Wanna learn?"

"I only have one available hand to use." He wiggled the fingers of his bad arm, which was in a cast from shoulder to wrist, completely immobile.

"That's all you need. Here, you play this key right here." Georgia pointed to a low C. "It will go with everything."

"Really?" He looked at her incredulously.

"Well, everything I'm going to play now." She winked, and watched as he moved to the bench, sitting sideways so his leg did not get in her way, being careful not to touch her. She scooted closer to him. "We are going to have to get cozy." Tyler inhaled her honeysuckle scent, and coughed.

At her command, he played the lonely C. Tentatively at first, then she gave him a beat and a tempo to keep. Before he knew it, she had broken out into a rousing boogie-woogie, fingers flying up and down the keyboard. He grinned, getting into the game. They laughed at the fun, Georgia making up multiple riotous melodies while Tyler played the single note.

"Okay. Now you can play one part, and I'll play the other."

Georgia showed him the bass notes to play in a repeating pattern. She played the upper keys with her right hand. This tune was familiar, but he couldn't name it. Then she smiled wickedly and wiggled her eyebrows, moving under his arm with her left arm to play more notes on the bottom keys. "Let's pick up the tempo."

Tyler lost focus and forgot his notes, his fingers tripping over each other. Georgia laughed again, sounding much like the tinkling of the upper keys she played. Clear and pure. He placed his hand lightly on her thigh. Georgia froze, looking down at the keys, then over at Tyler, trying to discern his meaning.

A thumping sound came from next door. It sounded like her neighbor was beating on the wall with a cane.

"Sorry, Mrs. Carson!" Georgia yelled through the wall. Her lips turned up and her eyes twinkled.

"That was fun, but maybe you should consider switching to guitar." Tyler smiled, moving back to his chair. Who knew he would enjoy that so much? He was not a singing cowboy. But when he finally went to sleep later that night, he dreamed of emerald green eyes, a tinkling laugh, and a singing piano.

* * *

ON MONDAY, Tyler said goodbye to his physical therapist, watched him leave, and heard him talk to someone on the sidewalk. There was a knock at the door, and a short gray-haired lady peeked in. "Hello?"

"Hi," Tyler responded. "Come on in." He had no idea who this was. He hoped she wasn't the little old lady from next door that they disturbed with their music.

"Hello, young man. I'm Mrs. Carson." She had a pie in her hand. Great. She would butter him up, then lecture him. He straightened in his chair and mentally prepared himself. She closed the door after entering.

"After hearing Georgia play her piano yesterday, I thought I should be neighborly, and maybe a little bit nosy, so I brought you a pie. You like pecans? They are plentiful in this part of Texas."

"Yes. That is so thoughtful of you. Please, come in Mrs. Carson. You can set the pie on the dining table. Pecan is actually my favorite." It smelled heavenly—the blend of sweet, syrupy goodness and flaky pie crust, made his mouth water. Maybe this lecture wouldn't be so bad after all. There was a pecan grove on the ranch. He would make sure she got some when they harvested in the fall. He moved his chair to the dining table.

Mrs. Carson placed a piece of pie in front of him that she had put on a paper plate, which she had also brought over, along with a plastic fork and napkin. She was watching him as he savored the sugary dessert for a few minutes. He closed his eyes in sheer pleasure. Wait. What was that flavor?

*Is that bourbon in the pie?* Tyler wanted to ask her, but when he opened his eyes, he saw that she was looking him over.

The older lady took a good long look at him, her intelligent eyes assessing. The bruises on his face had spread over the left side, turning a rainbow of colors that were fading out to green and yellow. His broken nose had been reset as much as possible, but there would probably be a ridge in it for the rest of his life. The casts on his right leg and left shoulder still rendered him mostly immobile, making him look more like a stick man than a strong, virile cowboy.

He wanted to ask if he passed inspection. Instead, he stuffed his mouth with the last bite of pie. Finally, she spoke.

"I've never heard Georgia play like that. It was a happy sound, even if it was loud."

"Yes, ma'am. I just asked if she could play, and that is what she came up with. She wasn't even using any music."

"Yes, she is very talented." She paused and locked her eyes with his.

"Now..." Her voice was stern. Here came the lecture. He was sure of it.

"Young man, I just want you to know how much we love Georgia. She is sweeter than that pecan pie you are eating. What are you doing here? Should we be shooing you away?"

She was getting right to the point, but he liked that about her. He looked up from his pie and grinned, feeling a bit like a little boy with his hand in the cookie jar. The pie was really good. He reached for a napkin and hoped he didn't have any on his chin.

"Mrs. Carson, look at me. Do I look like I am able to take advantage of Georgia?" He waved his hand up and down over his body.

Mrs. Carson chuckled thoughtfully. "No, I guess not. But maybe she is taking advantage of you." She lifted one eyebrow, but there was a smile with it, and maybe a hopeful glint?

Tyler tilted his head and raised his own eyebrow before taking a quick swig of the glass of water that she had set in front of him.

"Really, Mrs. Carson? I guarantee, there is nothing happening in this apartment that I couldn't put on social media. G-rated all the way." He waved his glass in the air. "Besides, I should be able to leave in a couple of weeks. Until then, I promise to be a perfect gentleman. Ma'am."

He twinkled his eyes at her. "By the way, is that lard in this crust? It is so good."

Tyler's grandmother had been a champion pie maker back in her day and had taught him a thing or two. They discussed pie recipes for the next hour before Mrs. Carson stood to leave.

"You should know, Tyler, we love Georgia and try to look out for her. She's lonely, and we would hate to see her do something she would regret." Mrs. Carson laid her hand on Tyler's arm. It was an innocent gesture, but he got the feeling she was sending a message. He just wasn't sure what that message was.

After she left, Tyler thought about what she had said, and two words stuck out in his mind. "She's lonely." Georgia is lonely? With all her activities, that is the last thing Tyler would have expected to hear. But maybe he had just learned something new about the beautiful, green-eyed teacher.

* * *

THE NEXT DAY, Mrs. Houston, the neighbor from the other side, came over with a peach pie. Her husband had been a direct descendent of Sam Houston, President of Texas after it won its independence from Mexico and before it became a state. She was proud of her heritage and told anyone who would listen.

She knocked on the door right after the therapist left. She must have been watching from her window. Opening the door as if she lived there, she peeked in, just as Mrs. Carson had done the day before. "Hello?"

"Hey there." Tyler noted the blond hair. Most older ladies were covering their gray with something more youthful. It suited her. "Come on in. I'm Tyler."

"I'm Mrs. Houston. And I must say, Mrs. Carson was right. You've got more plaster on you than the Statue of Liberty." She grinned as she said it, placing her pie on the table. "Do you like peach pie?"

Tyler's mouth was watering. "Peach pie is my favorite." He winked. "But don't tell Mrs. Carson. She thinks it's pecan."

"Well, her pecan pie is good. But my peach pie is better." She looked at him, almost studying. Tyler ate his piece, waiting for what she was going to say. He finally decided to answer the question he figured she was going to ask.

"There is nothing going on here, Mrs. Houston."

"How did you know I was going to ask that?" The older woman tilted her head.

"Because Mrs. Carson already did."

"Ah. Well, what I want to know is, why not?" A smile split her face.

Tyler coughed and worked hard to keep from spitting out his pie. "Excuse me?"

"You have the perfect opportunity. Georgia needs a good man. And I do love me a good love story." She wiggled her eyebrows.

Shaking his head, Tyler finished his pie before he spoke.

"For starters, Sam would kill me."

"Oh, yeah. Right. Sam." She raised one eyebrow. "Did you and Sam really duke it out in the parking lot of the Farm and Ranch Store?"

"I wouldn't put it quite like that."

"Well, I heard it was an epic battle. Blood everywhere." She spread her arms wide.

"You heard wrong, Mrs. Houston. He slugged me in the nose. Once. That was it."

"Well, did you at least deserve it?"

Tyler tapped his fork on his empty plate. "I guess I did. I don't know."

"That's my boy." She patted him on his good arm and winked at him.

These women. What was he going to do for the next few weeks? They seemed to be at odds on how they thought the relationship with Georgia was going. Or should go. But the truth was, it wasn't going at all. And couldn't. He needed to remember that.

When Mrs. Houston left, she promised to check on him in a couple of days. Tyler definitely felt like he was under inspection by the nosy neighbors. He hoped he passed. He would welcome one of those blue USDA stamps. Maybe he would get it tattooed on his arm.

•———————•

ON THURSDAY, Georgia came home to find both neighbors visiting Tyler together. They were laughing at some story he was telling. She felt a bit jealous.

"Yeah, the porcupine did get a couple of jabs in, but the cow kicked it and sent it tumbling across the field. You should have seen it rolling!" The three of them laughed together. "The poor cow had some quills stuck in her nose, though. Looked like she was trying to grow a beard. I had to pull them out with pliers. Poor thing bawled the entire time."

"Wow, looks like I missed the party." Georgia walked toward the dining table and set down the small bag of groceries she had bought on her way home, scanning her eyes over the food already there.

Tyler twinkled his gray eyes at her, then launched into another story. "Then there was this armadillo, and you know how they roll themselves up into a ball to defend themselves? Well, this little guy was all rolled up, and the cows were kicking it back and forth like a soccer ball. You should have seen it!" They all roared in laughter.

"Okay. Now I know you are making that one up. Texas armadillos don't roll up into balls. Only South American armadillos do that."

"Ah, come on, teacher, you're spoiling my fun." Tyler smirked.

She turned back to the group and smiled, noticing the empty plates and pie pan. "Apple pie? And ice cream? Ladies, you are going to have Tyler rolling around like that poor armadillo!"

"I beg to differ, madam!" Tyler flexed the muscles in his one good arm. "I am as fit as ever." He struck half a body-building pose from his chair as he said it.

Georgia's two neighbors giggled like school girls. Had Tyler been flirting with them? They seemed to be enjoying it.

"You know what? We should bring our quilting group over some day to keep him company. You know what we call ourselves, right?" Mrs. Houston winked at Tyler. "We're the Happy Hookers."

"Mrs. Houston! You did not just say that!" Georgia turned just as pink as Tyler was turning.

"Well, we make rugs as well as quilts. Didn't you buy something at our most recent bazaar? It was the brown and blue crazy quilt, as I recall." Georgia turned a brighter shade which creeped down her neck.

"Is that the one on my bed? It is kind of crazy, but I like it, especially now that I know who made it." Tyler was teasing her now, wiggling his eyebrows at her.

"I had been using that room for an office, so I hadn't really decorated it yet, and you needed something. I just thought the colors would be acceptable. That's all."

The ladies left another hour later, after an evening of "Back in My Day" stories, where the ladies talked about how things were different when they were younger. They all laughed together, the ladies sharing knowing winks and smiles. Georgia wasn't sure what some of that was about, but it was a fun night. She thanked them as she walked them both to the door.

"That's a nice young man you've got there, Georgia. Reminds me of my Mr. Carson. He was so much fun, and so sexy!" Mrs. Carson put her hand over her forehead and pretended to swoon.

Georgia coughed. "He's not my young man, but I appreciate your comments and your pies."

"Oh, but he is very smitten with you." Mrs. Houston patted her hand. "Every time he looks at you, it is like he wants to kiss you silly. Makes me wish I was a few years younger." She fanned her face with her hand, her eyes closed as if dreaming of days gone by.

Georgia rolled her eyes. "Good night, ladies. Will you come again next week?" Georgia tried to squelch their suggestions.

"We'll be here, darling. Wouldn't miss this for the world. How does blackberry cobbler sound?" They all laughed and her neighbors left, arguing over who got to make the cobbler.

Georgia went to her room and looked into her mirror. What did Tyler see when he looked at her? She wasn't drop-dead gorgeous like the woman who had literally turned his head that day on the square. She didn't have startling blue eyes like she read about in her suspense novels. Her face was average. She didn't have curves in all the right places. Oh, her figure wasn't bad but she was short and slim, if you liked pixies. And, of course, there were some standards that she refused to compromise.

She glanced down at Lily, who had strolled into her room like a queen. She shook her head and sighed, realization hitting her. Geez. She had turned into a cat lady.

The trickle of emotion that had started the day she blocked his truck with her car was building. She was afraid it would turn into a flood. Was he really smitten with her? Could there ever really be anything between them? No. Not in their present circumstances. Still, she was glad that she could help him, and that he was accepting her help. That had to be it. He was simply grateful.

# FIFTEEN

TYLER SAT at the dining table, eating the lunch that Mrs. Houston had brought by earlier in the day. The two ladies had become regular visitors.

"Hello? Anybody home?" Tyler winced when he recognized Ellen's voice. He knew she didn't like him.

"Come on in, Ellen. The door is open." He might as well face the music.

Ellen entered, carrying the car seat that held her four-month-old son. She walked to the table and sat the carrier down on the opposite end from where Tyler was sitting.

"Georgia's not home yet. Probably still at school. But she should be here in about an hour or so." Tyler held a spoonful of chicken and homemade noodles, which he stuck in his mouth and savored.

"I'm here to see you, Tyler. I just want to check in and see how things are going." She unbuckled her son from the car seat and lifted him into her lap. Tyler noticed he looked just like Sam.

"Things are going well. Therapy is going well. I'm hoping to be out of here in the next week or so."

Ellen studied Tyler. "That probably won't happen. Just saying."

"Why would you say that?" Tyler looked back at Ellen.

"Just being realistic. You have a lot of injuries. They are going to take time to heal." She bounced her son on her knee.

"Is there something I can do for you? You said you came to see me." Tyler tried to figure her out.

"No. I just wanted to see how things were going." In other words, she was checking up on him. She grabbed a napkin from the table and wiped drool from her son's face before tapping him in the nose with the napkin. The kid giggled, and Ellen did it again.

Tyler watched the interchange between mother and son. He had purposely avoided falling in love. But watching them together now, Tyler wondered what it would be like to have a son who looked just like him. He could lose his heart to that in a New York minute. Sam was a very lucky man. The thought scared him.

The front door opened again, and they heard Georgia calling Ellen's name. "I saw your car in the parking lot. Is everything okay?" Georgia walked into the room, a slight look of panic on her face.

"Yep. I just came by to. . ."

"Check on things." Ellen and Tyler both spoke at the same time. Georgia laughed at the stricken look she saw on Tyler's face.

Georgia put her bag down and picked up her nephew, snuggling him close. "Oh, you are such a beautiful boy! Yes, you are! Yes, you are!"

Tyler looked away. Was he jealous of a baby? The thought made him nervous.

Georgia and Ellen visited for a while before Ellen finally left.

When she walked into her galley kitchen, Tyler followed her and switched to a closer chair, preferring conversation over more television.

"Did you ever have a serious boyfriend?"

She looked at him curiously before lifting her head in thought. She seemed to be thinking about how to respond. Or maybe she was remembering someone. She shrugged, turning her mouth up in a slight smile. His heart skipped a beat at her faraway gaze.

"There was one guy in college. We hung out together a lot, but I wouldn't call it serious."

"Why not?"

"We wanted different things. He was going to law school after we graduated, and then I moved here with Ellen and Sam. He's probably a hotshot attorney in Houston or Dallas by now. Do you want something to drink? I've got sweet tea in the fridge. I made it this morning."

"Sure. That will be fine." He watched as she filled a glass with ice and the tea, setting it on the table in front of him with a napkin. He picked up the salt shaker and poured some onto the napkin, setting the glass of tea on top.

"Why did you do that?" She motioned toward the tea.

"Oh. It's just a habit, I guess. The napkin serves as a coaster, and the salt will prevent the glass from sticking to the napkin. I learned it in a bar somewhere."

"Okay. Well then. I just learned something new." She turned back to the kitchen.

"You didn't want to get married? To the dude?" The words were out of Tyler's mouth before he could stop them, going back to the subject.

Georgia tilted her head, considering the question. "I don't

know. Just never met the right guy, I guess. He wasn't the right guy. I know God has a plan for me out there somewhere, and I trust Him with that. In the meantime, I'm happy where I am and how I am. What about you?"

She had turned the question back to him, but he didn't want to answer it.

"Do you really think God cares whether you get married or not?" Tyler didn't think God cared much about him at all.

"Of course, He does. There are lots of verses in the Bible about God caring for our future, planning our steps—lighting our way. He made us, after all. Why wouldn't He care?" Georgia walked into the kitchen and opened the fridge again, pulling out meat to prepare for supper. She gathered an onion and potatoes from the pantry.

"And you think it's that simple? Seems kind of naïve, to me."

"Remember when we talked about Psalms? The night of the moon?" She lit one of the gas burners and placed a skillet on top with a dab of butter in it.

"Well, yeah. That was one incredibly beautiful and frustrating night, and I'm really sorry about it."

"Stop apologizing. Anyway, Psalm 139 says we are fearfully and wonderfully made. That all our days are written in His book before we are even born." She cut up an onion and threw the pieces in the butter.

He watched her from where he sat, resting his head on his hand. She had said something about that the night they watched the moon together. A night that ended in disaster. "Exactly. If everything is preordained, then why does God care what we do?" He took a sip of tea. "This is really good, by the way." He tipped the glass toward her in acknowledgement, then took a full swig, draining a good third of the glass.

"Thanks. Let me know when you are ready for a refill." She

paused, then spoke again. "God doesn't make our choices for us. We still have free will. He just happens to know what we are going to do before we do it. Didn't your grandmother or your mom ever tell you not to touch something hot, knowing you were going to do it anyway?" She handed him a sack of small red potatoes, a cutting board, and a knife. "Here. I think you can handle cutting some of these up for me. Please."

"Okay. But I still don't get it." He pulled several potatoes out of the bag.

She shrugged, as if she easily accepted the concept. "God knew we were going to have potatoes for supper tonight. But He isn't going to cut the potatoes up for us. We still need to act, make a choice, and do something, so that we can have potatoes for supper. You are providing the hands that cut up the potatoes. Or hand, as the case may be."

"Okay. What does this have to do with getting married?" Since he was one handed, he had to cut carefully to keep the potatoes from scooting off the cutting board as he cut into them.

"Because God will allow us to meet people we might fall in love with, but He won't necessarily walk us down the aisle. Not us," she pointed between the two of them quickly as she blushed. "But a proverbial us. You know what I mean." She turned back to her skillet and dropped a hunk of hamburger in it, hiding her face. Then she picked up the potato masher.

"Are we having mashed potatoes tonight?"

"No, we are having sloppy joes. I'm using the potato masher to smash up the hamburger so it will cook more evenly."

"Okaaayyy." That made absolutely no sense to him, like using a butter knife as a screwdriver, which his grandmother had always done.

"So tell me then." He scooted the pan of cut up potatoes over to her and she set it on the stove, adding water, salt and butter. Ingredients.

"What would be 'the right guy' for you? What would he look like?" He really should find another topic, but he was curious.

She shrugged her shoulders. "I don't know. I've never really made a list."

"What? I thought all girls had a list of what their dream guy would look like." He was walking through a mine field and he knew it, but he couldn't stop himself. He tapped his fingers on the table to steady his thoughts.

"Not me. But if I had to say—he would be nice. He would be kind to everyone. Respectful. I guess that would be number one." Georgia turned down the potatoes which had come to a boil, her cheeks turning red. "Simmer down there, girl."

"Huh? What did you say?" He thought he had heard "Simmer down there, girl."

"Oh, I just told the potatoes to simmer down." Now her cheeks were glowing, but that could be from the steam. She picked up the kitchen towel from the oven handle and wiped her forehead with it. He decided to change the subject back to cooking.

"What are you going to add to the hamburger?"

"I get a specific barbeque sauce from the store. I also add several spices to flavor the hamburger, some soy sauce, and a little bit of beef broth. I'll stir it all in here in a bit. When the potatoes are done, it will be time to eat."

• •————————• •

GEORGIA FINISHED THE MEAL, and set the food on the table and thought about their conversation. Her heart had jumped a beat when he asked about her wish list for a man. She immediately thought, "He would be tall, good-looking in a

rugged sort of way, outdoorsy, ride a horse, wear a black hat..."
She had to hide that thought quickly and hoped he didn't
notice.

She wondered further about their conversation about God.
What had made him so cynical? Was there something in his
past that had turned him away from God? Or had he never
known God to start with? Georgia knew a lot of her students
didn't have Christian parents. Maybe Tyler had been raised in
an unhappy home. He said he had no family except the grandmother he had mentioned a few times. She assumed the grandmother was no longer alive. And what was God's plan for his
life? It made her consider her role in that plan a little closer.
Was she interfering? Was she making things sloppy, or
mashed? Or both?

# SIXTEEN

A COUPLE OF DAYS LATER, Tyler came out of his room to see Georgia standing near the couch with a strange look on her face.

"Your phone rang. It was laying on the couch so I reached to pick it up, thinking it might be important. I thought for sure the screen said 'Mom' before it went black. But you said you don't have any family."

"Must have been a robo-dial. Maybe it said Spam." He settled onto the couch and slid the phone into his shirt pocket without looking at the missed call.

"Well, whoever it was left a message. I heard a beep afterwards."

"Yeah, I get a lot of calls like that, especially at this time of day."

Georgia looked at him sideways. He had a feeling she didn't quite believe him. He simply shrugged his one good shoulder and picked up the remote to scan for an action movie. He wasn't ready to divulge his past, and he knew she would keep digging if he let her.

The next day, Georgia walked into the living room and stood in front of the couch with a pile of clean washcloths in her hand. She had the kind of look that said she didn't believe the dog ate his homework. His leg was propped on the ottoman, and Lily was lying with her head draped over his cast. The cat was annoying, but he didn't have the heart to kick her off. And he would have to use his other foot to do that, anyway.

"Tyler." She tossed the wash clothes next to him. "Something has been bugging me for a while now."

He clicked the remote to mute the TV and picked up a cloth to fold one-handed. Then he stared back innocently, a question mark for an eyebrow. "What's been bugging you?"

"Your middle name. Someone at school said that you only had initials, but no name. I have heard some of the women around town call you Tall Black Hat Guy. As in your initials. TBHG. Or at least, that's what I have heard. And it fits, since you only wear that beat-up black hat. It kind of has a reputation of its own, you know." She paused, then added, "And before you ask, my name is Georgia Nicole Duncan. Now. It's your turn." She wiggled her eyebrows in jest, those beautiful green eyes twinkling, her dimple deep in her left cheek.

Since Tyler had come to Nora Hills, nobody had asked him about his middle name. It was like everyone had the feeling that it was a sticky subject, and nobody had the nerve to approach him about it. Especially since he had two initials. Most people only had one. Leave it to Georgia to open that barn door.

"Why does that bug you?" He tried to toss the question back to her.

"Because despite what you said yesterday, I know it was the word 'Mom' displayed on your phone when it rang. It was a really cute ring, too. Not like your normal country twangy ringtone."

Closing his eyes, Tyler breathed in deeply, then sighed.

The programmed ringtone for his mother gave him away. This was a part of his life he never talked about.

"It's a long story." He tried to stick with his standard reply. Only Randall Hudson knew his full story, and that was because he had ties to his family's business. Nobody else in town knew his history, and so far, it had stayed that way. But after a couple of weeks with Georgia, it didn't surprise him that she would bring it up again after that phone call. She was tenacious.

"We've got time. All day, in fact." She sat down on the ottoman, scooting the cat out of the way. Lily jumped off and went to the cat tree.

He focused over Georgia's head to look out the window, tossing his options back and forth in his head. He really preferred for his story to remain private. But she had been very gracious to him, and he felt like she deserved to know. Would she keep it secret? He decided to trust her.

"I'll tell you, but it stays between us. You can't even tell Ellen or Sam. And definitely not the gossip mill at school. Or your church." She nodded, her face serious. "No one from the meal train. Not Mrs. Carson or Mrs. Houston, even though they are sweet little old ladies. They will be telling all their friends. It'll be worse than TikTok. For all I know, they have their own channel.

Georgia chuckled, but it wasn't funny to him. She frowned when he did.

He took a deep breath.

"I'm adopted." She widened her eyes as he spoke. "I was named after my adoptive grandfathers. And you're right. It's a pretty stuffy name, which is one of the reasons I don't use it unless I'm signing a legal document."

He paused, and Georgia waited. He picked up another washcloth and folded it, giving his hand something to do. He didn't know how to explain without her getting the wrong idea about him.

"My grandfather on my mother's side was named Harriman. My grandfather on my father's side was named Boseman. I think they thought that having the family names would help me fit in better. They were wrong."

Georgia's eyes lit up in recognition. She held an index finger in the air, squinting as if in thought. "Wait a minute. Your full name is . . . Tyler Boseman Harriman Grant? Are you related to *the* Bosemans? Of Boseman Corporation in Utah? Oil and natural gas Bosemans?" Georgia pointed her finger at him. She didn't look happy when she saw the confirmation on Tyler's face. But he wasn't very happy, either, as he saw and heard her mental wheels spinning.

"Your family is as rich as Croesus. They have holdings all over the world." She stood, and her arm flailed as she spoke. "Not just oil and gas, but silver, copper, and diamond mines. We did a case study on them in science one day." She paced back and forth, her gestures telling him he was in trouble.

"Why would you let me believe you have no family? You lied to me." She paused, as if another thought had occurred to her. "Do they even know about your accident?" Her hands went to her hips and she stared down at him, demanding an answer.

He shook his head. This is exactly what he was afraid of. "It's not like that, Georgia. I'm not rich. My family is." He looked at her with a slight frown. "And to set the record straight, I have never said I have no family. I said I have no family to speak of."

"That's a matter of semantics. And why don't you speak to your family?" Georgia crossed her arms again and raised one eyebrow, frustrated. She clearly expected him to explain more.

Geez. Was this what it was like to be one of her students? He would take a day pushing cattle in the hot sun over her stare.

"I didn't lie, you just assumed." He fidgeted in his seat. If she had on glasses, she would be looking over them.

"You know what? I'll just leave." He waited a moment then continued. "I'll call Mr. Hudson and go back to the ranch. He said I could stay in the guest house." He folded the last cloth and put it on the stack. The stack fell over.

Tyler didn't want to leave, but he wouldn't stay if she truly was that upset with him. He really liked her. There was a charge between them, like the static in the air before a thunderstorm. But their attitudes about life were worlds apart. And he had made a promise to Sam, anyway.

Lily sensed the tension between them and jumped off the cat tree, racing into Tyler's room. The cat had adopted him, no matter how hard he tried to discourage her. He would be picking cat hair off his pillow—again.

Georgia watched the cat run, then sat down on the ottoman again and laid her hand on his cast. He looked at her hand, wishing he could feel her soft fingers on his leg. He shook his head to refocus on the discussion.

"You don't have to leave, Tyler. But I don't understand." Georgia spoke quietly.

"I was three years old when my parents adopted me and gave me my name. I don't know what it was before that." He shrugged, then winced at the pain. He needed to stop doing that. "But I always felt different from the biological children that my parents had after adopting me. There are seven of us, you know. It was a crowded house. Anyway, they like biscuits and gravy. The creamier, the better. I don't. I like sour foods. They don't. I have gray eyes, all of them are brown-eyed. I'm rough around the edges. I like the outdoors. They are more refined and disciplined. Studious. Some have musical talent, like you. I don't."

He hung his head. "I know they love me, and I love them, in my own way. But I just don't fit in."

"Does Mr. Hudson know?" Her question made him look up.

"Yes, he and my father have some business contracts together."

"And that's how you got down here? From Utah?"

"I was only going to stay a year, then go home. But I liked it, and I'm good at it, so I decided to stay. And, I like the independence of being my own man. Even though I live in a bunkhouse.

Look, you and Mr. Hudson are the only two people who know. And I would like to keep it that way, please. I haven't even told Reggie, and he's my best friend on the ranch. Don't look at me like that." She had opened her mouth to speak, but shut it. "When people find out who I am, they treat me differently. I just want to be Tyler."

She nodded before asking her next question.

"Why do you wear that beat-up black hat? You can surely afford something better?" She pointed to the hat sitting next to him on the couch.

Tyler's gray eyes turned to steel, throwing his head back in a huff. "This is why I never tell anyone about my family. People automatically want to make me fit into their idea of what a member of an affluent family should be like. What we should wear and how we should act. It's one of the reasons I left home and came to Texas. To get away from that. We're not like those rich and famous families on television."

"I didn't mean it that way. I was just curious. Is it something special to you?" She stared at him, waiting. It made Tyler squirm, but he nodded.

"Actually, it was my father's hat. He gave it to me when I left. To remind me that I have a family, is what he said. I just like the feel of it. It's old and worn and fits the shape of my head." Tyler restacked the folded washcloths on the couch. He needed a distraction.

"You didn't answer my other question." Georgia pressed him, but her tone was soft. "Have you told your family about your accident?"

"No. I will. When the time is right."

"They deserve to know. Your mom deserves to know." She nodded at his shirt pocket, where he had tucked his phone.

"If I told Mom, she would be flying down here and taking over everything. I don't want that, and I don't think you would, either." He looked pointedly at her. "Worse yet, she would probably hire a private air ambulance to take me home. And I definitely don't want that. I would be stuck there for eternity."

"She's your mom. She loves you." Georgia spoke softly.

Tyler closed his eyes and sighed. He was tired of this conversation. "Give it a rest, Georgia. I will tell them. When I decide. Case closed." Tyler picked up the remote, turned off the muted television, and moved into the wheelchair. The discussion was over.

# SEVENTEEN

ON SATURDAY, nobody came by to help, and Tyler was on his own while Georgia made her weekly grocery run. This had become his normal Saturday morning for the past three weeks. Sitting on the couch, leg up on the ottoman, pillows under his injured arm, watching educational shows. A man who claimed he could paint an entire picture in thirty minutes was painting another mountain. He had painted a different mountain every week.

Georgia walked into the apartment, took one look at Tyler, and giggled. He had a pencil in his good hand, trying to twist his arm around his back.

"What's so funny?" Sometimes he wasn't sure if she was laughing with him or at him. And they had kind of avoided each other since their blow-up earlier that week.

"Sit up."

"Why?"

"Just sit up. I'll scratch your back for you."

"How did you know I was scratching my back?"

"Because I use a pencil for the same thing. Lean forward."

"Getting bossy, aren't you?"

"Well, I am a teacher." She scooted to the small space between Tyler and the arm of the couch, bending one leg next to his so she could reach his back. Flexing her fingers, she scraped her nails up and down over his muscles.

"To the left, just a little." Tyler twisted while she scratched. "Oh, yeah. Right there. Scratch. Scratch hard." He flexed while she dug her nails into his back.

"Now who's bossy?"

"Well, I am the patient."

She scratched his back for a couple of minutes, chasing the phantom itch as it moved from side to side. He enjoyed the feel of her fingers as they roved over his back. She had a magic touch with her hands. And maybe he milked it, just a little bit.

"That's enough. Thank you, Georgia." Tyler sat back and picked up the remote. Georgia stood and cleared her throat. A pink blush graced her cheeks.

"What's wrong, now?"

"Um, your shirt. It's crooked. Do you want some help with it, too?"

"What's wrong with it?" Tyler looked down. The sleeve had been cut out so he could get it over the cast on his arm. He wore scrubs for pants. He couldn't wait to get back into his jeans.

Georgia went to her room and came back with a hand mirror.

He took in his reflection and grimaced. He thought at first, she might have been talking about his face, but the bruises were healing nicely. Then he glanced at his shirt, which he had snapped together crooked. Snaps were easier to manage than buttons, but they were still difficult to do one-handed. And he wasn't a Prima Dona but his clothes had always fit perfectly. Since the accident he felt like he had become a slob.

"Um, sure, thanks. You can help if you want to." He blew out a breath. The tension between them was still a little thick.

Georgia sat on the ottoman, but needed to get closer, and his leg was in the way. He patted the couch next to him again, his request silent. They had just sat closely, but this time they were face to face. Tyler held his breath. He knew she felt the attraction between them, just like he did. Her face turned rosy, the color spreading to her ears and neck. He hoped he didn't have the same look. That would surely give him away. But he couldn't stop watching her. Her eyes were fringed by long, thick lashes. Her hair was up in its usual ponytail, the smell of sunshine buffering the sweet scent of her honeysuckle shampoo.

• •————————• •

GEORGIA SWALLOWED, suddenly nervous. His eyes had turned cloudy. Gray and smoky. He had some stubble over his jaw and chin this morning and she could see a small mole on his face that she hadn't noticed before. There was nothing fancy about him. But her heart still thudded in her chest.

"You wanna just unsnap the whole thing and start over?"

His eyes said so much more, his gaze steady, his gravelly voice creating a sand tornado in her mind. There was way too much to unpack in that question. Was he talking about the shirt, or about them? Her fingers itched to find out.

She avoided his gaze and focused on fixing the shirt. He had skipped the top snap to leave it open, so she reached for the first snap on one side, unsnapping it to line it up with the correct snap on the other side. She got a glimpse of his chest when she did. No T-shirt for Tyler, with his arm and shoulder bound up. His skin was still tan, as if he spent a lot of time in the sun bare-chested.

She focused on the next snap. She was over his heart, and she could feel it beating erratically. Her own heart beat in time with his. She breathed in to compose herself, catching more of his scent. She smiled faintly and worked on the next snap.

"You know, I could have just worn it crooked all day."

"You're right, Tyler. But, um, it would have bugged me to death." She kept her head ducked, focused on the snaps. *Breathe, Georgia. Just breathe. Nope. Don't inhale. Just breathe. In and out. Steady. That's right.*

"And what about it would bug you? Hm?" He tucked a small lock of hair behind her ear, and raised her face with a finger under her chin to capture her eyes. There was a hint of fire behind the smoke, his eyes becoming more heated. She looked away, then turned back to his shirt to focus on the task at hand.

She had to do the next snap three times before it clicked, her cheeks turning red and her hands trembling. When she reached his flat, narrow stomach, Tyler laid his hand on top of hers.

"That's fine. Thank you." He pulled the last two snaps open so they would line up, and let the shirt hang.

"My pleasure." The phrase had rolled off her tongue before she could stop it, warm and breathy. Georgia looked up at him then. He was looking at her lips, and they were so close. Then realizing how her words sounded, she hid her eyes.

"It was my pleasure, too." His voice was right in her ear. Warm, and...

Oh, boy. She wanted to fan her face.

"You know what I mean. You're welcome. Or whatever. *Crud.*" She said that last word under her breath, but she thought he heard her anyway. Totally embarrassed, her neck turned red. She heard him chuckle as she scooted off the couch and nearly ran to the kitchen to put the groceries away.

She stood in the kitchen, staring out the window at nothing in particular. Her arms were crossed over her middle, her heart pounding in her chest. Lily rubbed against her legs, and she picked the cat up, cradling her to her face, enjoying the softness of her fur, and rumbling purr.

She had thought this would be easy. He would be here during the day while she was at school. They would have minimal contact except on weekends, like today. And she was just being friendly and helpful. She had no ulterior motive for him being here, right? But she would need to be careful. She was like the fly, being drawn to him inexplicably. And he was the spider, spinning his web.

Why did she want him here? She hadn't tried to explain it to herself, but if she had to be honest, she was lonely. Even though she had a cat, she wanted to come home to the sound of life. Instead, it had been the sound of silence until Tyler moved in. But having him here was starting to get just a bit uncomfortable. They were going to get on each other's nerves.

She would need to look for more ways to fill in the time. Perhaps the youth group at church would be willing to help. A visit from them could prove to be entertaining. And what could happen with an apartment full of kids as chaperones?

SUNDAY MORNING, Georgia went to church and arranged for a group of kids from the youth group to come over to entertain Tyler in the afternoon. They played a long, intense game of Monopoly while Georgia watched. Since he was the math whiz, they made him the banker, but they quickly found out that was a mistake. Before they knew it, he owned Boardwalk, Park Place, several other high-dollar properties, and all the railroads, with hotels on each. He effectively bankrupted them one at a time. He didn't even land in jail. Not one single time.

"Where did you learn how to play Monopoly like that? Emily asked the question. She had just turned fourteen, having had a birthday. Tyler confessed he received his MBA degree from Utah State. He could have gone into finance, but he chose to be a cowboy instead.

Another one of the kids asked, "But if you're so good at math, and you actually like it," the student shuddered, "why would you want to be a ranch hand?"

Tyler smiled as he answered. "Have you ever tried to count cows?"

Jimmy shook his head. "I just live in a small apartment with my mom and brother."

"A cowboy is responsible for keeping track of every cow in the heard. If you lose even one, that can be a lot of money. And when you're responsible for a thousand head of cattle—and remember, a head can include a mama and her calf, so that's really two—you need to be good with numbers."

The boy scratched his head. "I never thought about it that way. Will you still be able to count the cows, with bein' all busted up like that?"

Tyler looked at Georgia before facing Jimmy again.

"Well, you know, Jimmy, sometimes things happen in life that take us down a road we didn't think we would take. We make plans, but then something like my accident happens and causes a detour. You have to roll with the punches. But my doctor says I'll be fine."

Tyler had asked that question of himself quite a bit lately. He had his MBA, after all. He knew he wasn't cut out to be a bean counter, which some of his friends had called his degree, but was counting cows enough? And was he rolling with the punches, or fighting the inevitable?

Tyler knocked twice on the table, a gleam in his eyes. "How about another round? Anybody game?" Everyone groaned, and the doorbell rang. It was the pizza they had ordered, and the distraction gave Tyler a moment to think. He watched the kids as they crowded around the pizza, cheese dripping in lazy strings as they moaned in delight over the number one teenage meal.

Anything multiplied by zero, is still zero. And right now, Tyler felt like that big fat round number. *If you're so good at math, why are you a ranch hand?* The question bugged him. He had been saving his pay for the past nine years and investing most of it. What he hadn't used for partying, at least. He didn't have a thirst for money like his adoptive father did. But he did start to see the value of planning for a future, and already had a sizeable nest egg. Still, would he want to be a ranch hand all his life? If not, what would he do? He was thirty-three. Long past time to be making decisions.

Truth was, his father had seen his talent and wanted to bring him into the family business, wanting to groom him to take over some day. But Tyler did not want to become a corporate executive. He loves the outdoors. He plays at math for fun. He knew people couldn't or wouldn't understand. So he left Utah, moved to Texas, and found his job at the Double H, which now had a contract with Boseman Oil & Gas. There was a freedom here that he would never find back home. But a cowhand? That was not good enough for Georgia. He was not good enough for her. She deserved more.

Georgia had ordered several pizzas from Pamela's Pizza, family-owned and operated with the best pizza in town. Tyler immediately picked all the mushrooms off of his slices.

"Eew." He grimaced, the expression almost making

Georgia laugh. "I eat enough dirt on the ranch. I don't want it on my pizza." Tyler searched his large piece to make sure he got all the offending fungi off the slice.

"Fine. Next time I'll get it with anchovies." Which drew another look of horror from Tyler, and a smile from Georgia, complete with cute little dimple. That made everyone laugh, but many of them also made faces that looked like they had just eaten sour lemons.

The kids took turns signing his casts before they left, some signing his leg, others signing his arm. A few got creative, drawing silly faces and other emoticons that they all used on their social media posts. Emily drew a picture of a cat's face. The rest of the kids simply signed their names, or wrote "Get Well."

When the parents arrived to pick up the kids, they finally said good night to everyone and Georgia closed the door. But Tyler didn't want the night to end, so he handed the marker to her, wiggling his eyebrows.

"Let's see what you can come up with, Shortcake."

"You want me to sign your cast?"

Tyler looked into her green eyes, which had grown wide, his lips turning up into a slow grin. He could easily get lost in them. "I dare you to come up with something witty."

He challenged her with his gaze, and waited as she thought for a moment, tapping the marker on her lips. She looked upward for inspiration.

Tyler relaxed against the couch and patted the seat next to him, inviting her closer. She sat on the edge of the seat and he urged her closer, tapping his arm.

"Put it right here, so I can see it every day."

He would give anything to be that marker right now. He could see the wheels turning in her mind as she was thinking about what to write. Would it be serious? Funny? Simple? Or maybe just her name. But there wasn't much room left since the kids had covered most of the cast. Finally, Georgia turned on the seat, reaching across his lap to get a better angle, and wrote something short, blocking his view with her head. He inhaled her honeysuckle scent, itching to run his fingers through her shiny auburn locks as they spilled over her shoulders.

When she handed the marker back to him and started to get up, he reached for her wrist and pulled her back to face him. Then he looked at the letters and numbers she had written on his forearm.

"SOS 8:7? What does that mean?" Tyler was puzzled.

"Not telling." Her voice was musical. "That will give you something to figure out while you are recuperating." She danced away while she spoke.

"Save our Ship? Are we drowning? Or is it just me, drowning in your deep emerald pools?" She had given him a riddle to solve. And yeah, he said that last part out loud.

"You are such a flirt. SOS can mean other things too." Georgia dared him to think further. But Tyler was truly stumped. His brain would likely mull this over while he slept. Would they be pleasant dreams, or nightmares? He hoped it didn't mean 'Same old . . .' Well . . . you know.

••————————••

"MISS DUNCAN, are you and that Tyler guy going to get married?"

Georgia choked on the water she had just sipped from the bottle she kept on her desk. "What gave you that idea, Jimmy?" He was the kid that had asked Tyler why he was working on a ranch, and was one of her students. His math scores had gone up since the night the youth group had visited.

"Well, you are living together. At least, that's what my mom says."

"No, we are not living together. He can't go back to the ranch until his leg and shoulder are healed, and I have an extra room, so he is staying with me. But we are not living together." She emphasized that last part again.

"You were making moony eyes at each other last week when we came over for Monopoly." Jimmy demonstrated by twisting his eyes together with an exaggerated sigh, and some of the kids laughed at his antics.

"It takes a lot more than moony eyes," Georgia imitated Jimmy's expression, "to make a marriage." The kids laughed again, but she could tell they were all listening to her answer. Whatever she said would go home to the parents. She was sure of that.

"Tyler will be going back to the ranch soon. I'm just doing my Christian duty to provide him with a place close to town while he heals. Close to the doctors and therapists, and such."

Georgia admitted the thought had crossed her mind. But Tyler was not the type to settle down. Their relationship, or lack thereof, was just another in his string of flings. Even if it was innocent. But Jimmy's question caused her to pause.

Living together? A lot of people lived together these days. Not that she would do that herself. She believed in the sanctity of marriage. And her relationship with Tyler was platonic. Very platonic. No sparks, no steam. Yep. Uh-huh.

Jimmy's mother, and anyone who would listen to her, just needed to mind their own business.

# EIGHTEEN

FRIDAY NIGHT AFTER SCHOOL, the meal train from the church had ended, so Georgia brought home barbeque from Wing and a Prayer. The meal included an assortment of meats including beef brisket, chicken, and pork. Baked beans with bacon and brown sugar. Baked macaroni and cheese, and something called 'dirt' for dessert, which looked like chocolate pudding with crumbled cookies and whipped cream. She had texted Reggie for ideas, and he said brisket was Tyler's favorite food. She included sweet tea for both of them.

"Shortcake, I love you! My favorite place!" Tyler reached for the large bag Georgia had carried to the table and took out several boxes. "Best wings this side of Heaven!" was printed on the top of one box. "Our brisket is divine!" was printed on another one. The third one said, "Our pork is purely providential!" The smell of the smoked meat and tangy sauce permeated the room.

He reached into the brisket box with his hand, scooped up a hunk, and stuffed it into his mouth, moaning in delight. She melted inside. He had said he loved her, but she knew he was talking about the barbeque she brought home. Still, she wondered what it would be like to do this every night. Share their meals together. Talk about their days. Long walks at sunset. Picnics on the lake. She stopped and shook her head. She was dreaming. It could never be.

She set the rest of the food out so that Tyler had easy access. The meal included several side dishes. Macaroni and cheese and baked beans, but also sour foods like slaw, olives, and pickles. His eyes lit up at the sight. This was a side of him that she was sure few people knew existed. He was like a little kid, enjoying his favorite food. He was not the rogue that rumors said preyed on women. He was funny, sweet, and kind. He was appreciative of everyone who had come by to visit him. And as much as she didn't want to admit it, she had fallen so hard she didn't think she would ever be able to get back up.

Tyler shifted his leg as they ate, a pained look crossing his face.

"What's wrong?" Georgia had noticed a glint in his eyes.

"I have been hurting most of the day. Just a dull ache in my joints. Can you get some ibuprofen for me?"

"Sure thing. You know, my grandmother used to be able to tell the weather by how she felt. She always knew when it was going to change." Georgia imitated her grandmother's voice and bent over like she was using a cane. "I can feel it in my bones." She wasn't really making fun of her grandmother. She had loved her with all her heart.

Georgia handed him the pills, her soft fingers grazing his calluses when she placed the pills in his hand. She drew away quickly, and wondered if he had felt the same zing that she had. She sat down in the chair across the corner from his.

He swallowed the pills with a sip of tea, then reached out for Georgia's hand again. Leaning forward, he stared into her eyes, his own grays turning darker.

"What do you feel in your bones, Shortcake?"

Georgia started at his question. What did he mean? Was he talking about physical feelings, or something more? She was feeling a lot of things, but not in her bones. When he looked at her the way he was looking at her now, it sent heat straight through her to her gut. She tore her eyes away from his handsome face. He hadn't shaved this morning, and it made him look like a hero from the romantic suspense novels she liked to read.

"What do you mean?" It was a whisper.

"Well, for instance, this barbeque." He dropped her hand and picked up another piece of brisket, dangling it in front of his mouth. She wondered if he knew how sexy his voice was, setting up that swirling anticipation that pulled her in.

The meat continued to dangle in front of him. "I love brisket. And I love to savor it. I love its smell, the promise of the enjoyment I will get when I eat it, and the explosion of smoky juiciness in my mouth. I *feel* the flavor before I eat it. What do you feel?" He devoured the piece in one bite, his eyes twinkling, drawing her attention to his lips.

Was he saying what she thought he was saying? Good grief, it was getting hot in here. She tugged at her blouse, blinking as she did to clear her thoughts.

"I feel like we had better eat up." He had gone from being the little boy with his favorite food to being full blown scorching hot in sixty-seconds flat. Her heart raced like a herd of horses flying across a wide-open plain.

He grinned at her and raised his eyebrows, as if he knew the effect the conversation was having on her. They were sitting at the corner of the table, across from each other. He reached around the corner and grabbed her chair, pulling her, chair and all, across the tile floor and around the table, closer to him. Being laid up for weeks hadn't dulled his strength at all. Nope.

"Do you feel this?" He ran the back of his fingers down her arm, from her short sleeves to her wrist. He smiled when the goosebumps popped up, while Georgia cringed. She couldn't deny the attraction.

"Tyler. . ." He was so handsome. Those gray eyes and strong jaw were attractive enough, but when you added in the slight ridge in his nose and the wave of hair falling over his face she wanted to swoop in and kiss him.

He moved his hand to her face, touching lightly under her chin to tilt her face to his. He caressed her cheek with the same feathery touch he had caressed her arm with.

"Do you feel this?" His voice was softer, his eyes gentler.

"Tyler . . ." She froze. She should stop him.

He leaned in, moving his hand to the back of her head, pulling the band out of her ponytail before cradling her head in his hand, his mouth close to hers.

"Do you feel this?" The question was just a whisper, but it reverberated in her soul. She took one solidifying breath.

"Tyler. I don't want to do this."

That stopped him cold in his tracks, his eyebrows scrunching together. "You don't want to?"

"We can't." It was that simple. They could not allow anything to develop between them while he was living there. Her heart pounded.

Thunder rolled outside and dark clouds closed in, looking ominous. Storms gathered quickly in this part of Texas and could turn violent. He studied her face and she hoped her expression mirrored what she was saying. Her eyes drooped with sadness. He dropped his hand to his side.

"You're right, Georgia. I'm sorry. It was my mistake." He pushed her chair away, with her still sitting in it.

They finished the meal quickly, and Georgia gathered the now empty boxes. She looked out her picture window and watched as the wind began to blow the small trees outside her apartment sideways. Rain soon began to splatter, the large drops plopping as they hit the pavement.

Suddenly, the rain turned to small frozen pellets, bouncing as they hit, and then to pea-sized hail. Georgia and Tyler snapped their eyes to each other. They both knew what this meant.

"Power may go off soon. We might have to hunker down. Do you have any candles? We should get them ready." Tyler looked around him.

"I don't know. I'll have to look." Just as she said that, the lights blinked, then went dark.

Tyler picked up his phone and turned on the flashlight. They stared at each other as the storm continued to howl, and he could see the concern in her face.

"Are you okay?" Tyler's voice was strong, while she felt weak.

Shaking her head, Georgia cleared her thoughts. "I just don't like storms." She turned away from Tyler before speaking again. "I think I still have an oil lamp that was my grandmother's." Georgia turned in a circle, her hand to her chin in thought. "It might be on the top shelf of the kitchen cabinet." She was glad for the distraction. She had to focus.

She walked into the kitchen while Tyler held the light for her and followed behind. There wasn't much room in the galley for his chair but he maneuvered as closely as possible.

She pulled out a folding step stool, set it in front of the cabinet, and began to climb. Since she was short, she wasn't even able to reach her middle shelves without assistance. Tyler wheeled his chair behind Georgia to hold his light for her and to spot her.

"Don't want you falling in the dark." His voice was rough.

"If I fall, I'll hurt you." And she didn't want to do that.

"I'll catch you, either way. But please don't fall."

She stepped from the stool onto the counter in order to reach into the back of the top cabinet shelf.

"I found it. And it has oil in it. It must be several decades old. I hope it's still good."

Tyler chuckled. "Old lamp oil is made from kerosene. It won't go bad. If there is a problem, it will be with the wick. Hopefully, it is still immersed in the oil and hasn't dried out."

Georgia retrieved the lamp and leaned over to set it on the counter beside her feet. She climbed off the counter and down the stepstool to the floor, grinning triumphantly. "Let's take this to the dining table. Oh, wait. We need something to light it with."

"Do you have a lighter that is used for the little round grills?"

Georgia rummaged through her kitchen junk drawer. She grinned, holding it aloft like a magic wand. "Let there be light!" She needed to find a way to bring back the mood they had enjoyed earlier in the evening.

Within minutes, they were basking in the warm glow from the oil lamp. It cast flickering shadows on the walls, creating a scene that would be romantic in any other setting. The storm continued to rage outside. But there was another storm raging between them. Gray eyes locked with green. He had almost kissed her just a few minutes ago. Georgia looked away first, a pale blush on her cheeks. Would he try again?

She shoved her thoughts aside, looking for another distraction. "Let's do a round-robin story. I have done this before in one of my classes to fill in time. We can even record it and add to it from time to time if we want to." They had to do something productive or she was afraid she would be the one to give in.

"How would that work?"

"I'll start the story with a few details. Then it will be your turn, and you will add some more details. The crazier, the better."

"Okay. I'm game. It will give us something to do."

"Great. Let me open the voice recorder on my phone." She sat her phone in the middle of the table. "I'll start."

"Once upon a time, since all great stories must start that way." Georgia wiggled her eyebrows. "Once upon a time, there were two kingdoms. One was at the bottom of a hill, and was called the Kingdom of the Maggies. The other one was at the top of the hill, and was called the Kingdom of the Aggies." Georgia stared expectantly at Tyler. "Okay. Your turn."

Tyler turned his head to think, twisting his lips sideways as he did. She hoped he would make this funny.

"And the Maggies were long, spiraled springy creatures." He imitated the movement of the springs as his hand boinged up and down on the table. "While the Aggies were round like a marble, rolling everywhere they went." He held his hands in front of him, as if he were driving.

For the next hour, they went back and forth, building a story about two warring kingdoms that came together after one of the most precious Aggie tots had to be rescued by the fiercest Maggie warrior, when it had rolled down the hill and couldn't get home. They laughed uproariously as the story unfolded, becoming more ridiculous with each turn they took. And in the end, it took them both by surprise. Because they realized they had told a story of two people who had absolutely nothing in common, yet still needed each other.

They stared at each other as the story ended, Georgia's phone still recording. They both reached for it at the same time, and his hand covered hers. It was still raining, but the storm had subsided, and the rain was now a gentle shower that lulled away her defense.

The lamp flickered its light against the wall. Their two shadows stared at each other, mocking them as if to say, *"What are you waiting for?"* The light danced between them, taunting them with its glow. *"Go on, you know you want to."* Her hand developed a mind of its own. Against her will, she turned her palm up, taking his fingers in hers. She licked her lips and he leaned closer, his eyes searching hers.

"You've heard of the olive theory, right?" His question took her by surprise and she held her breath.

"If a guy likes olives, or pickles, and the girl doesn't, it means they were meant to be together."

"What if it's the other way around?" She teased, knowing he was the one who liked sour foods. She preferred creamy things.

"Same result. And it's just you and me here tonight, Short-cake. Think we should test this theory?" He spread a lock of her hair around her shoulder.

His voice drew her in. She reached out to him tentatively, grazing the fingers of her other hand across the fingertips on his injured arm, marveling at the calluses that were still there. He was a working man, with strong working man's hands.

She heard him draw in a quick breath, surprised at the intimacy they felt. Who knew such an innocent touch would cause such a reaction? She traced his jaw with her thumb. It was turning a more normal color, the bruises healing. She ran her finger across the bridge of his nose. The break there hadn't affected his handsome face at all. He sat there in silence, eyes closed, barely breathing.

He opened his beautiful gray orbs and lowered them to her lips, leaning into her touch. They were barely an inch apart, and they both knew they would connect this time.

"Georgia . . ." His lips whispered against hers.

Georgia's phone rang, blaring loudly. "We Are Family," an oldie's song from Sister Sledge, made them both jump apart. Tyler pulled back with a groan, dropping his hand. Georgia turned her head away, embarrassed. Jumping up quickly, she ran her hand over her hair. Where was that scrunchie?

"It's my sister. I need to answer this." She grabbed the phone to silence the ring.

•——————•

TYLER SMILED AT THE IRONY. Couldn't Ellen have waited another minute or two? He leaned back in his chair and listened to Georgia's side of the conversation as she paced the living room.

"Yes, Ellen, we're fine."

"No, we don't need anything."

"A substation, huh?"

"All night. Yeah, we'll be fine."

"Yes, I know not to open the refrigerator and let all the cold air out."

"No, we had brisket. Yeah, it was pretty good, except for the sour coleslaw."

Tyler started boxing up the leftovers from their meal. There wasn't much left to save, so he gobbled the last two pieces of brisket. It was still good, even though by this time it was cold. He gathered everything together into one box so it would fit easier in the trash can. When he wheeled back to the dining table, Georgia was still talking.

"No, you don't need to come over."

"It's getting late. We'll probably just turn in."

"Yes, Ellen. To our separate rooms."

165

"Sheesh. You're not my mother."

"Goodnight, Ellen."

Tyler rolled his eyes and shook his head with a grin at the conversation, then silently blew out the oil lamp. He would use the flashlight from his phone to light their way down the hall. The night could have gone much differently. Too bad Ellen had to call and interrupt them.

"I guess it's time to say goodnight. Let's leave the lamp here so it can cool off." He started toward his room.

"Goodnight, Shortcake."

"Goodnight, Crip."

Back in his room, Tyler took another deep breath and let it out slowly. Her nearness and the sweet intimacy of the night nearly undid him. Honeysuckle, green eyes, dimple, ponytail, and everything else about her screamed that she was beyond him.

He had wanted to pull her into his lap and kiss her until she begged for more. He ran his hand through his hair, which was hanging in his eyes now. He was starting to look more like a rock star than a cowboy. He would need a haircut soon, but he was not going to let her do that. He was afraid that would be the last straw. He absentmindedly rubbed Lily's fur as she sat next to him on the bed.

It would be very easy to fall in love with her. She had taken the time to find out his favorite foods, which he found endearing. She defended him when Sam complained about his being here. She ignored the rumors, even though he knew they had to hurt. She even held him accountable when she found out he hadn't told his parents about the accident. If he was honest with himself, he had fallen for her a long time ago. But he wasn't willing to admit that.

"DO YOU PLAY GUITAR? I looked around, but didn't see one anywhere." Tyler's question brought her head up.

They were sitting at the dining table the next morning, eating sausage and veggie omelets. Power was restored during the night, and sunshine was shooting a beam through her kitchen door, dust motes floating like fairies. She distracted herself as they ate by surfing through online shopping sites, trying not to think about their near-kiss the night before.

Georgia squinted her face and wondered at his train of thought. She was glad he hadn't mentioned last night's storms. Plural. The storm outside, and the storm that had also raged between them inside. She had spent much of the night tossing restlessly. But maybe he hadn't felt anything at all. Maybe she was just another girl to him. Maybe it had all been a game.

She blinked to come back to the present. "No, I don't play. But I have always wanted to learn. We had a neighbor when we were growing up who taught piano, and I found it came easy to me. Plus, our piano was my grandmother's small upright, the one right here, so we didn't have to buy one. But there was no one around who taught guitar lessons, and that was extra money that my parents didn't want to spend, anyway. Not that we were poor. It was just unnecessary." She shrugged.

"I bet you could teach yourself. There are all kinds of online videos for that now. You don't even need a nosy neighbor." He nodded at the wall Mrs. Carson had banged on the day they were playing the piano.

Georgia laughed. "In case you haven't noticed, I don't have a guitar. I would think that would be the first requirement."

"You know, I haven't forgotten about last night." His soft

comment came out of nowhere. He met her eyes when she looked at him again.

"I haven't, either."

# NINETEEN

TYLER WOKE UP GRUMPY. He had been unable to sleep, tossing and turning as he thought about the night earlier in the week when it had rained, and their two near-kisses. When he finally fell asleep, the dreams started. He was on Cap, pushing cows around, but Cap turned into a giant wheelchair and the cows turned into mice, a calico cat chasing them all around the field.

Georgia had gone to school and he had slept late. He looked around his room, at the scenery that hadn't changed in more than three weeks. Growling to himself, he wheeled to the living room to look out the large window there. Georgia didn't even have a patio he could sit on. He was losing his tan. He was a cowboy, for Pete's sake. He spent all day in the hot sun, he and Cap and the guys, pushing cattle around and mending the fences that kept them inside their boundaries.

Now he sat in air-conditioned comfort, and except for his injuries, he was getting soft. He had to get outside.

He could call Reggie, but he knew they were all busy since they had to pull his share of the ranch duties, too. His casts still prevented him from driving, and he hadn't been cleared by the doctor anyway. Besides, his truck was now sitting in the junk-yard or had likely already been crushed. He couldn't even beg a ride from Georgia. They had already proven her car was too small. He could call a ride-sharing service, but he would still need his wheel chair since he couldn't walk.

Flipping through the TV channels, he saw a commercial for a car rental agency and an idea struck him. His insurance would pay for a rental vehicle, and this agency would deliver the car to him. He picked up his phone, hoping he was not over-stepping. Georgia may not be happy with this idea.

·•————————••

GEORGIA RETURNED HOME from school to find a new SUV in her parking spot. She parked next to it, fuming. Couldn't they see the word RESERVED painted on the pave-ment? She got out of her car and walked into her apartment to see another man sitting there with some kind of tablet in his hand.

"Oh, hey, Georgia! This is Joe." Tyler pointed at the other man. "We're renting an SUV." His face was lit up with excitement.

"We're what?" Georgia raised her eyebrows. What was Tyler up to now?

"I've got to get out of here, Georgia. I can't stay cooped up inside any more. So I'm renting an SUV, and you get to drive. Joe needs a copy of your license, then we are done."

"Tyler, we don't need to rent an SUV." Joe stopped typing at Georgia's response and looked up.

Tyler laughed. "Come on, Shortcake. You remember that night, don't you? There is no way I will fit in your tiny green stink bug, especially with these casts on my arm and leg. My insurance will pay for this."

Georgia blushed as Joe looked at her, obviously amused at Tyler's mention of 'that night.' Great. Another rumor. This one will float around the car rental dealers and will likely be highly embellished.

"Well, I do suppose you are probably tired of looking at my bare walls. This way, you can help me with my grocery shopping."

"Deal. And we can also go to the Blue Bull. Sit on the deck. You can meet some of the guys from the ranch."

Georgia handed Joe her license, which he scanned into his tablet. Tyler initialed "here, here, here, here, and here," and finally signed his name. Within minutes, a driver in another SUV pulled into the parking lot, and Joe was gone.

When Georgia offered to let Tyler stay with her to recuperate, she thought it was just going to be a couple of weeks. She had no idea she would become his chauffeur, to the Blue Bull, no less. She would ask Sam and Ellen to meet them there as backup. She had a feeling she was going to need the support.

Three hours later they were at the bar. They pulled into the handicap parking spot in front of the outdoor deck and were immediately surrounded by five rowdy cowboys led by Reggie. Two others were on rotation back at the ranch.

The group led them to some tables that had been pushed together and were already set up with beer at each seat. They pulled back one of the chairs and wheeled Tyler into place. "It's party time!" one of them shouted. Tyler introduced him as Ritz.

"No beer." Tyler pushed the longneck aside and turned to the waitress, who had quickly joined the group, sidling up to Tyler. "I'll have a root beer. Georgia, what do you want?" He knew she wouldn't drink, even if she wasn't driving.

"I'll take a sweet tea, please." Sam and Ellen were not drinking, either. The waitress ignored them and flirted with Tyler.

"Whatever you want, sugar. You know I deliver." She winked at him, right there in front of everyone. Georgia fumed.

"And let's get a round of sides. Nacho Mountain, and fried mushrooms and zucchini sticks. Georgia, do you want anything else?" Georgia appreciated that Tyler was trying to send a message to the waitress, who was bending over the table to enter the order into her tablet. She provided everyone with a nice view of her bountiful blessings.

"Wait." Ritz looked at Tyler funny. "No beer? I thought you came here to cut loose and have fun."

Tyler shook his head. "I'm wobbly enough as it is, since I'm still trussed up with limited mobility. I don't need a wobbly brain, too. Besides, Georgia has already seen me drunk once before. I don't think she wants to see that again." They had all heard the rumors that had flown through town about the teacher and Tyler going home together. Georgia's cheeks turned a rosy blush.

Roundabout was a new group in the area and had taken the stage. They played a variety of music, mostly designed for country line dancing, but included some classic rock and ballads as well. Georgia tapped her foot as they watched the dancers from their table on the deck.

The group of cowboys took up most of the outdoor space. Girls swayed by their tables, seeking attention and making salty promises with their winks. Georgia was silent about it, but Tyler mostly ignored them. Instead, he kept his focus on her.

The guys were merciless as they teased Tyler about becoming henpecked. They knew that was not the case, but there was some thread of truth about them settling in. He locked his eyes with hers and barely raised an eyebrow, his grin pulled sideways for a brief moment before turning back to his cohorts. Tyler had once told her the guys all thought she was cute. She wondered what they were thinking now.

Reggie pointed at Georgia's head bobbing and foot tapping to the music as the band played. "How's about taking a swing with me around the dance floor?" He stood and held out his hand to her.

She looked at Tyler, then at Sam and Ellen who nodded, then back at Tyler who frowned. Finally, she looked back at Reggie, who had a wide grin on his face and a twinkle in his eye. Was he trying to make Tyler jealous? Georgia took his hand, and they joined in the line dancing.

•——————•

"FESS UP, TYLER," Ritz said as soon as they left the table. She's taking care of you, right?" Ritz wiggled his eyebrows, his implication clear. "I wish I had a cute little chick like that taking care of me." He turned his head back to watch as Reggie led Georgia to the dance floor.

Ellen frowned. Sam cleared his throat. Maybe Ritz didn't understand that Ellen and Sam were Georgia's sister and brother-in-law.

Tyler shook his head and looked sternly at Ritz. "That was uncalled for, Ritz. Yes, she is taking care of me, but not in the way you've implied. I think you owe Sam and Ellen an apology," nodding his head toward them.

"Really? What's happened to you, man? You're no fun anymore. I guess I'm outta here." He pounded his fist once on the table, stood, and left. He didn't apologize. Tyler blew out a breath and looked at Sam and Ellen, who were looking back at him with question marks in their eyes. Tyler just shook his head. Would the insinuations never end?

"What do you do while Georgia is in school? It must get pretty boring with no cattle to push around." One of the other cowboys asked the question as they all watched Ritz leave.

"She has two neighbors that come over from time to time."

"You mean the little old ladies? You must be slipping, man."

"Nah. Actually, they are a lot of fun. And they bring me pie." Tyler wiggled his eyebrows.

"I heard you had a visit from the Engleman twins." The guys all smirked at him.

"They brought by a casserole. And I sent them immediately home. So if you heard anything else, it is a flat-out lie." Tyler squished his napkin in his fist.

"All right, man. Don't get defensive." The cowboy held his hands up in surrender.

But Tyler was tired of the rumors.

Thirty minutes and a lot of two-stepping later, Reggie returned a laughing Georgia to the table, his hand on her waist where he had held her for most of the dances. Her face was flushed and her eyes sparkled. "That was fun, Reggie. Thank you so much!"

Reggie tipped his hat. "Sure thing, darlin'." Looking back at the crew still sitting around, he said, "I'm cuttin' out of here, guys. I've got an early morning." He smiled knowingly at Tyler. "Take care, man. We'll see you when you are back to work. Then I'm taking a long vacation." He walked away whistling, his I-just-danced-with-Georgia-and-you-didn't swagger, teasing his best friend.

"What was that all about?" Tyler had a sour look on his face as he turned to Georgia.

"What do you mean? It was a dance. It was fun." Everyone watched their exchange.

"Tyler, man, cut her some slack." One of the other cowboys spoke. "She has been taking care of you for several weeks, as you just pointed out. She needs her fun, too."

The music stopped while the band took a break. The air around them stilled. Even the birds had stopped singing. Tyler looked around, realization hitting him. He lifted his beat-up black hat and brushed his too-long hair back before settling the hat back on his head. "You're right. I'm being selfish. The truth is I wish I could be out there dancing, and Reggie was just rubbing it in." He adjusted his hat on his head again.

Sam laid his hand on Tyler's shoulder. "You'll get there, man. Doc says another week or so, right? In the meantime, you don't have to wait for Georgia to take you anywhere. You've got friends."

Friends? Tyler hadn't exactly thought of Sam as a friend. More likely a guardian over his wife's little sister. Not too long ago the man had slugged him with a crowd of people watching.

"Thanks. I appreciate that." He looked around, ready to lighten the mood again. "All right! Who's up for another round of sarsaparilla? I'm buying." They all laughed and cheered. Tyler hadn't had a drop of alcohol since his accident, and most of their bottles sat unopened as well, in tribute to his return to the fold.

It was after midnight when they arrived at the apartment. Georgia helped Tyler into his chair and pushed him through the door, heading for his room. He reached his free hand over his shoulder, behind him, toward Georgia. "Let's talk for a minute."

Georgia walked around the chair to face him and sat on the couch.

175

"I just want to thank you. I don't think I've done that yet." He really did mean it.

Squeezing his hand, she nodded. "I'm glad I can help. I don't think either one of us really thought through what we were getting into when we decided to do this. But I'm glad we did, regardless."

"And we've got an SUV for at least the next two weeks. We can get out and do things. If you want to, of course." He let his smile slide up to his eyes.

"Of course. You've been cooped up for far too long." Georgia's smile turned into a yawn. She started down the hall.

"Goodnight, Shortcake."

"Goodnight, Crip."

Tyler watched her walk to her room. Was that all this was? Was it about her helping him? Could she be offering more? Did he want more? And what would people be saying about them now that they had gone out in public?

* * *

GEORGIA LAID in bed and stared at the ceiling as she thought about the last few hours at the bar. She and Tyler hadn't gone together as a couple, but it almost seemed as if Tyler had wanted to. She was surprised at the way he reacted after she danced with Reggie. The fire in his eyes and accusatory tone had been unexpected.

She experienced her own pangs of jealousy at each woman who sauntered by their tables. From the waitress taking their order to the groupies that hung around the cowboys, each woman had cast a longing eye at Tyler.

How many of these women had been up on the hill with him at some point? How many had he kissed? Or more? She knew his reputation, but she could see part of that was due to the number of women who threw themselves at him. How many of the stories about him were actually true? Tyler had not flirted with any of the women tonight. His smoky eyes remained focused on her for most of the evening.

Ignoring the late hour, she picked up her phone and dialed Ellen.

"Hello?" Her sister sounded sleepy.

"Oh, I'm sorry, Ellen. I guess I sometimes forget you have parents' hours."

"Parents' hours?"

"Yeah. An early bedtime."

"It's okay, Georgia. Is something wrong?" Georgia could hear footsteps followed by the clinking of a coffee mug.

"I don't know. I just thought it would be nice to talk. We didn't really get a chance to do that at the Blue Bull tonight."

"Yeah. Those cowboys kept you busy. But this is not just a casual phone call. Not at this hour. Did Tyler do something?"

"What? No." Georgia looked at the time on her phone. Crud. It was almost midnight.

"Georgia. What did he do? I don't need to send Sam over there, do I?" Muted voices told her Sam was also awake and had joined Ellen in the kitchen. She could hear Ellen getting a cup of water from the refrigerator dispenser.

"No, don't send Sam." Georgia switched the phone from one ear to the other and sighed. "Actually, he hasn't done anything."

"Did he kiss you tonight? He seemed pretty focused on you, especially while you were dancing with Reggie."

"No, he hasn't kissed me."

There was a pause before Ellen answered.

"You mean he didn't kiss you tonight. Right?"

"No, I mean he hasn't kissed me at all. Well, there was the

kiss on the cheek after the fair. But that doesn't count." She stood and paced to her bedroom window, staring out into the night, behind the apartments. The sky was lit up by another full moon, bright enough that she could see a tomcat as it chased a female feline across the top of the privacy fence. The pair jumped off on the other side, their cries loud in her ears.

"I'm not sure I believe that. What about the night you watched the moon? And fell asleep together?" Ellen must be reading her mind. Georgia could hear the insinuation in her sister's words. But given the circumstances, it was a logical question, even if the night was innocent.

"He didn't kiss me then, either. He barely touched me." Of course, she wouldn't admit they had woken up wrapped together in the blanket. A scraping noise came from the hallway, and she glanced at her closed door. It was probably Lily, but she still lowered her voice. "I'm telling you, Ellen. It was nothing."

"What about the night you went home together? From the bar? A lot of people saw you leaving together. I'm not sure they believe that he slept on your couch." Georgia could hear the skepticism in Ellen's voice. She could almost see her sister's raised eyebrows.

"He was drunk, Ellen. Nothing happened. At all." She caught herself, glancing at her door again, and lowered her voice. Doesn't Ellen remember how Tyler went to the church and told everyone what happened? Or more importantly, what didn't happen?

"Really, Georgia? You expect me to buy this? Especially since you woke me up in the middle of the night?"

"Maybe his reputation is all fictitious. Maybe people don't really know him."

"And you do?" The question hung between them.

"He has been a perfect gentleman, Ellen." Georgia flopped back on her bed.

"Then what's the problem, Sis?"

What's the problem, indeed. Ellen didn't understand. Then again, Georgia couldn't really define the problem, either. Maybe she was simply longing for something she couldn't have. Her biological clock was ticking, leaving her head and her heart at war with each other.

Sam Jr. cried in the background. Georgia heard footsteps as the cries grew louder. She said goodnight to her sister and pulled the covers over her head. When she finally fell asleep, she dreamed she was dancing with a tall, faceless cowboy in a beat-up black hat.

# TWENTY

THE NEXT FEW days flew by. Tyler went with Georgia on her trips to the grocery store, driving one of the electric carts so that he didn't have to use the wheelchair.

They could have ordered online and used the pickup service, but that would defeat the purpose of getting out of the house. So they decided to simply smile as people nodded in greeting when they passed by in the aisles. Some stopped to ask him how he was doing and he shook their hands. Others watched him and Georgia as they shopped together. It was more fodder for the gossips.

He finally got his hair cut. Georgia grimaced as the barber ran his electric shears across Tyler's head, hating to see those luscious waves fall to the floor. He said it was getting shaggy but she said she liked the wild, rugged look it gave him and was sorry to see it go.

The barber winked at her and said "It'll grow back," but he did leave enough on top to let a wave fall over Tyler's forehead. It still gave her enough to play with, if she wanted to. Yeah, well, that wasn't going to happen, no matter how much she wanted it to.

They went once more to the Blue Bull. The ranch hands from the Double H met them there and encouraged Tyler to hurry up and get well. They missed him, of course, but they had also been picking up his duties in addition to their own and were looking forward to a return to normal. They also eagerly danced with Georgia, and were attentive and respectful as they twirled her around the dance floor. How much of that was out of deference to Tyler, she didn't know.

Still, she would love to have been able to dance with him. They had danced together when he was drunk, but that didn't count. She wanted to feel his muscular arms around her and his rock-solid chest under her hands when he was in complete control of his senses. She wanted him to twirl her in his arms, stepping around the dance floor and laughing together. And she wanted to sway with him to a slow beat, while he held her close. Oh, my, how she had fallen.

•———•

TONIGHT, they were at the Blue Bull again. Tyler sat at the same table on the outdoor deck where they had gathered before. He drummed his fingers on the smooth wood to the beat of the music and watched as Georgia danced with Ritz. Tipping his hat back, he brushed his fingers through his now short hair before putting the hat back in place.

"What's going on, Tyler? You're antsy tonight." Reggie pointed when Tyler picked up the salt shaker, passing it back and forth between the fingertips of both hands.

"Hm? I'm not antsy. Just ready to get back to life again." He set the salt shaker aside and picked up the pepper, shaking some onto his plate.

"You're putting pepper on your fries."

"Crud." Tyler pushed his plate away. He liked spicy fries, but not with black pepper on them.

"Something on your mind?" Reggie motioned for the waitress to take the plate.

Tyler narrowed his eyes. Reggie shouldn't pry. Cowboy code and all. Mind your own business. But Reggie and Tyler had been friends for years. Reggie could read Tyler just as easily as Tyler could read Reggie.

"Nope. Just itching to get back in the saddle." He was literally itching under his casts. Maybe that was what was driving him to distraction. Or maybe it was the little pixie dancing with Ritz, who was flirting heavily with her. She looked uncomfortable, but she was too polite to tell him to shove off.

THE NEXT SATURDAY AFTERNOON, Tyler flipped mindlessly through the TV channels. There was nothing on live TV except oldies, cartoons, and infomercials, and nothing that appealed to him on any of the streaming apps. The sports channels played baseball games, or talked about the upcoming football season and who was being traded, but Tyler wasn't a big sports fan.

Georgia was vacuuming the floor, dancing as she cleaned, earbuds in her ears so that she didn't disturb Tyler. Or maybe so that he couldn't hear what she was listening to.

She was dressed for cleaning house, in shorts and a tank top which accentuated her slim arms and shapely legs. Her shorts were . . . short. He had never seen her legs above her knees because she always wore skirts or jeans around him. He knew she didn't work out, but even though she was dainty, she was also well built and he liked what he saw. She could probably heft a fifty-pound bag of grain if she had to. Her hair was up in her regular ponytail. She never wore much makeup, but she didn't have any on her face today. He liked it. It spoke volumes about her confidence around him.

Tyler watched as Georgia danced. She had great rhythm and swung her hips in a pattern that reminded him of his sisters' dance team. He wondered what she was listening to.

"Hey. Are you gonna share?" Tyler watched her from the couch and waved his good arm to get her attention. She pulled one wireless earbud out of her ear and held it in her hand.

"What?"

"Are you gonna share?" Tyler tapped his ear.

"Share what?" She turned off the vacuum.

"Whatever it is you are listening to that is making you smile and dance."

"Oh. It's nothing. Just some oldies." Georgia shook her head, her cheeks turning a little pink.

"Give it to me, Shortcake." He pointed to her hand, palm up, wiggling his fingers. "I want to hear it."

"No." She closed the earbud in her hand and stood her ground.

Tyler raised his eyebrows. Now, this was intriguing.

"C'mon. I promise I won't laugh." He continued to hold his hand out.

"No way, Crip. You will laugh." Georgia's eyes sparkled. She stepped closer, teasing.

Laughter was the furthest thing from his mind.

"C'mere." He wiggled his fingers again, his eyes locking in on her beautiful green gems. *Come on Georgia. Just a little bit closer . . .*

It was the middle of the day. The mood wasn't romantic. The sun shined brightly through the windows. There was no candlelight or oil lamp burning, no shadows flickering on the walls, no thunder booming or storm bending the trees sideways. But he couldn't help himself any longer. Her mere presence beckoned to him, her dance moves making him ache to pull her in closer. Just one more step.

Before she could react, he wrapped his hand around hers and tugged. She landed with a plunk on the couch, almost in his lap. Their faces were inches apart.

"Hi." Tyler wiggled his eyebrows.

"Um, hi." Georgia froze as their gazes met, nose to nose.

"You look very enticing out there, dancing with that vacuum cleaner."

"Um, thank you?" She was breathless, and he knew it was more from their nearness than the vacuuming. He chuckled.

"Let's see what you are listening to."

"Nuh-uh." The look on her face told him it might embarrass her. Now, he was really interested.

"It can't be that bad."

She shook her head.

"Shortcake." He caressed her fingers. "What can it hurt?"

She opened her fingers, shielding her face as she did. Quietly, almost reverently, he took the earbud from her hand and plugged it into his ear. His eyebrows lifted, and his grin grew even wider when he heard Bonnie Raitt's sultry voice. "Let's Give Them Something to Talk About" sizzled in his ears.

She started to rise, and he caught her, sliding his hand around her waist, preventing her escape.

"You know, Georgia, you make me feel things I've never felt before. And it scares me."

Because he had been thinking about her. Every day since

he moved in. And those green eyes had haunted him more than once in his dreams. Knowing that she was sleeping in the next room made his heart race every night, restless with a want that he had never felt. It went much deeper than his normal nights on the hill.

Their entire relationship had been fuel for one rumor after another. Even now, he assumed that each visit from well-meaning folks resulted in someone making up a much-exaggerated version of what they had seen and heard. They had been out together in the SUV several times and he had seen the looks people gave them, the whispers behind hands that hid nothing. He didn't care so much about himself, but it wasn't fair to Georgia. She had been good to him. Good for him. And there was something cooking under the surface between them. It felt like applewood bacon frying in his soul. Sweet and salty.

The song changed to "Kiss You All Over." He caressed her jawline, his thumb sweeping softly over her cheek. Gray eyes met green.

"You have the most incredible eyes." He ran his index finger along the tiny line at the corner of her eye.

"You said that. The night at the bar, when you were drunk."

"I may have been drunk that night, but it's true. I have never seen eyes this color. They're straight from DaVinci's palette."

"Well, now you're exaggerating." Their faces were so, very, close.

"I'm completely serious. And your hair." He pulled the scrunchie, releasing her ponytail to let her auburn tresses flow over her shoulders. Holding it to his nose, he inhaled deeply.

"Honeysuckle. Just like what grows out at the ranch. You know, you can smell its sweet scent on the breeze at night. Makes me think of you."

"Now you are just trying to flatter me."

"And you sing with the voice of the whippoorwill in the twilight. Mellow and pure. Makes me want to keep listening and never stop. I still think of that song you sang to me."

"Tyler . . ."

"Sh-h-h." He placed a thumb over her lips, his fingers cupping her jaw.

"Do you know how perfect you are?" They were a whisper apart, so close he could almost feel her heart beating along with his own. Their scents mingled. Honeysuckle and cowboy.

An unspoken hope hovered between them. Her eyes closed in anticipation, her tongue moving subconsciously along her lips, against his thumb. The song continued to whisper to them.

"I'm not supposed to do this. I promised Sam. But I can't help myself. You'll have to tell me 'No'."

Static built between them as he waited. He watched her face, searching her eyes again for any further hesitation.

"Woman, you've got me flummoxed." He closed the distance.

When their lips finally met, they both felt the sparks. Weeks of anticipation brought every sensation alive. It was like rain on a tin roof, lightning and thunder in the distance. He wove his fingers through her hair, pulling her closer. She responded in kind. He would give anything to have been able to wrap both arms around her. He had never felt like this before. Not with any woman.

Georgia gasped as he moved his lips to her ear.

"You're so beautiful." She shuddered as he rained kisses down her neck to her shoulder.

"You're smart. Such a good teacher." Then back up again to her mouth.

"Funny." He slid his hand down her back, tugging closer as he did.

"Generous." She clutched the back of his shirt with one hand, and he let her pull him even closer.

"Creative." Her other hand wove through his black waves that the barber had left with a wink, just for her. He loved the feel of her fingers as they roved over his scalp.

"Heavenly." He pulled her brown waves over her shoulders, swirling them both in her scent.

"Delicious." He let his craving take over, finally tasting what had tempted him for weeks.

•———————•

GEORGIA'S TANK top gave him plenty of access to her neck and collarbone. Was this ecstasy? The room was spinning, but it felt so good. She shivered as Tyler left a trail of fire along her shoulders. How could she be hot and cold at the same time?

He groaned and coaxed her mouth open wider, pressing her back against the couch as he did. Georgia rode the wave with him, allowing him to claim her, answering with her own lips, abandoning any ideas of propriety. She admitted to herself that she had wanted him to do this since he had moved in. She reveled in the assault of his lips on hers. She had never been kissed by anyone like this. But this wasn't Anyone. This was Tyler Boseman Harriman Grant.

"I Feel the Earth Move Under My Feet." When did she add that song to her play list? Man, oh, man, her world was shifting right out from under her. His kisses were slow and sweet. Dangerously distracting. Tantalizingly torturous. Painstakingly perfect.

He had almost kissed her several times, but something had stopped them every time. This kiss was worth the wait. It was spectacular. Exquisite. Everything she had hoped for and more.

Even with a broken body, his lips and hands set her on fire everywhere they touched. She wondered about his injured arm and leg, but they didn't seem to bother him.

He plundered her mouth with his own, and she let him, new sensations galloping through her brain. His two-day stubble tickled, and she winced as he nipped the spot where her neck and shoulder met, just behind her left ear. He went back to her lips, capturing them again with vigor as she opened to him once more. Two more songs played, neither of them paying much attention to the music.

The thunder in her head pounded louder. One earbud was in his ear, the other in hers. The playlist switched to the next song. "I Heard it Through the Grapevine."

Georgia tensed. This was just temporary. Tyler was healing, and would be leaving soon. Her shoulders drooped, her hands pushing him away slightly. He was not hers.

Tyler moved away in response to her change in mood. He dropped his hand from the back of her head, releasing her as he did. He breathed in deeply, his forehead on her shoulder.

Time stilled, but only for a moment.

"I probably shouldn't have done that." He sat up, backing away as he did, his eyes sad. "But I'm not sorry I did, because every word I said is true. You are everything I could ever want in a woman." His soft whisper was like sandpaper. She looked at him hopefully, but it was dashed with his next words.

"If I could change the world tonight, our worlds, I would do it in a heartbeat. We would find a ranch somewhere and grow old together, surrounded by a bunch of rowdy kids. I'd give you the picket fence dream. I'd give you everything on your wish list."

He paused, and she waited.

"But I'm not the right guy for you, Georgia. I wish I was. Dear God, how I wish I was."

His look was so earnest, almost sorry, like he really believed what he was saying. He placed the earbud into her hand and closed her fingers around it, kissing her fingertips as he did.

"I really wish things could be different." He slid away to the other side of the couch and reached for his chair.

Georgia stared at him, her brain still fuzzy as she slowly came back to reality. When she blinked, her vision cleared.

"Don't I get to decide who is right for me? Maybe that's why God put us here together." She said it to his retreating back as he wheeled away. He had promised not to touch her, and he had just broken that promise. But he was also breaking her heart.

Georgia rose from the couch and closed her hand around the vacuum cleaner handle, sighing as she wound the cord and placed the appliance into the pantry where she stored it. Neat. Tidy. That was the way she liked things. But this situation was neither neat nor tidy. She looked at the couch where her scrunchie laid on the cushion, and frowned, touching her bruised lips with her fingers. His kisses had lit her on fire.

The song switched again, to "I Fall to Pieces." Georgia collapsed to her couch and pulled her knees to her chest as Patsy Cline poured out her pain. Tears pooled, falling down her face as her heart broke. Now what would she do? Her large apartment had suddenly gotten much, much smaller.

# TWENTY-ONE

FROM THE PRIVACY of his room, Tyler sent a message to Sam, asking him to come to the apartment while Georgia was at church on Sunday. He had to know what Georgia's note on his cast meant. She had told him she wouldn't explain it because it would give him a puzzle to solve while he was healing. But now he was afraid to discuss it with her. It might open up a line of conversation that he wasn't willing to have with her yet. Or maybe at all. Things had just become way too complicated.

"Maybe that's why God put us here together." His heart squeezed tightly in his chest at her words, the pain palpable. Does God really orchestrate things like that? Why would He even care? Tyler knew that living together, according to her standards, was a sin. But they weren't truly living together in that sense. Then again, after today, he wasn't sure. What were they doing?

Supper was quiet that evening. Tyler stayed in his room the rest of the afternoon and ordered pizza to avoid any further interaction with Georgia. One box for each of them to keep things simple. Reduce the possibility that she would expect him to eat with her. That would be awkward.

He had definitely crossed the line and didn't think they could go back to their friendly banter, so avoiding her was his best solution. He picked up the box that he had ordered for himself, placed that and some napkins on his lap, and wheeled back to his room, staying there the remainder of the night. Even Lily avoided him, choosing to stay with Georgia. He was truly alone with his thoughts.

Sunday morning, Sam knocked before entering the apartment.

"Hey, Sam. Thanks for coming over." Tyler sat on the couch with a cup of coffee in his hand. Lily was by his side, but moved to her perch when Sam came into the room.

"There's more coffee in the kitchen. Georgia made a pot before she left." He hoped he and Sam could put aside their differences today. It was time to bury the hatchet.

Returning from the kitchen with his mug, Sam sat down in a nearby armchair. "How are you doing, Tyler?" Tyler smiled at the genuine question.

He explained the visit from the youth group and how they had all signed the casts on his leg and arm. Sam had seen the writings when they were at the Blue Bull, but they hadn't talked about them. "Georgia also signed my cast, but she won't tell me what it means." He pointed to the space on his arm where Georgia had written the cryptic message.

Sam looked at Georgia's short scrawl and scrunched up his face in thought. SOS 8:7. With a smiley face in the O. He scratched his jaw.

"I have no idea what this means. Sometimes women do funny things that men can never understand. Ellen is the same way. It's like they have their own language and men aren't privy to their logic. But knowing Georgia, I bet it is from the Bible somewhere." Looking around, he spied her Bible lying on top of the piano. She had forgotten it this morning. "Pull up an Internet search app and look for 'SOS 8:7 Bible.' Let's see what it says."

Tyler entered the letters into his phone. "It says Song of Solomon 8:7 and it has a link. I don't know why I didn't think of doing this before." Tyler chuckled and clicked on the first link.

"*Many waters cannot quench love, neither can the floods drown it. If a man would give all the substance of his house for love, it would utterly be condemned.*"

He frowned. "What the heck does that mean?"

Sam cleared his throat, his elbows on his knees as he leaned forward. "Tell me the truth, Tyler. How do you feel about Georgia?"

Tyler turned his head and considered Sam's question. There was definitely a connection between them. But would it be enough to sustain a relationship? Tyler liked the party life, hanging out with lots of girls. Or at least, he used to. Georgia was pure homemade goodness. A chocolate chip cookie to his hobo stew. "To be honest, Sam, I'm not sure. She's an incredible woman. I'm just not sure I'm good enough for her."

"Well, based on this SOS," Sam looked him in the eye, "she seems to think that you are. I'd say the next step is yours." Sam placed Georgia's Bible in Tyler's lap and patted him on his healthy shoulder. "Is there anything else you need before I leave?"

"Yeah. A Guide to Understanding Women."

Sam laughed. "If you find one, get me a copy."

After Sam left, Tyler flipped through Song of Solomon, curious for more context. He went back to the first chapter and read more slowly. Wow. This was some spicy stuff. And this was in the Bible?

He found a ribbon bookmark and turned to that page. It was the story of David and Bathsheba. Now, that was a story he knew, remembering his grandmother recounting the tale while he was a kid sitting on her lap. But her version was tame compared to the version he found in the Bible. The room grew hot. He tugged at his shirt then picked up his phone again.

"Reggie? I need to get out of here. It's time to go back to the ranch. Can you help?"

•—————•

GEORGIA CAME HOME from school on Monday to find a ranch truck where the SUV had been parked. Tyler's duffle bag and hat were on the couch, and Reggie was helping him pack. Tyler hobbled into the living room. His casts were off, and he had a walking boot on his leg. His shoulder was bound in a sling and a swath ,but the cast was gone.

"You're leaving?" Georgia knew this day would come, but she wasn't prepared for it to happen today.

"Doc said I'm cleared to go back to work on light duty. There's a lot I can do from an ATV, and I need to get back to it. And you need your apartment back." He picked Lily up into his arms, cuddling her close and kissing the top of her head before setting the calico gently back onto the floor. Georgia's eyes filled with unshed tears.

"Were you even going to say goodbye? I would have fixed a dinner to celebrate getting your casts off. Or at least picked up some brisket." She swiped a tear from her face and scratched her neck, wincing when she noticed that the bandage was gone. She pulled her collar up tighter, looking around the apartment as she did. The wheelchair was gone, the piano and dining table had been moved back into place. It was as if he had never been here.

Tyler turned back to the couch to grab his duffle bag, throwing it over his good shoulder. Reggie took the bag off his shoulder and tsked.

After one last look around the place where she had opened her home and the façade around her heart, Tyler picked up his beat-up black hat and placed it firmly on his head.

"I really appreciate everything you and everyone else have done for me. But it's time for me to leave." She knew they were both thinking about that kiss. It had only been two days ago.

He stopped in front of her as he made his way toward the door, taking her face into his hands, and brushing his lips lightly against hers. She inhaled, wanting to remember him with all of her senses.

"Goodbye, Shortcake."

"Goodbye, Crip."

Tyler stepped out the door, ducking his head as he did, and she stood in the doorway as he climbed into the truck. Reggie lifted himself into the driver's seat with a small wave to her, and within a couple of minutes, they were gone.

Georgia closed the door and watched out her window as they drove away. The tears that had been gathering in her eyes slipped down her cheeks. Her heart was breaking, but she knew this had to happen. She sat down at the dining table, her head in her hand, and found her Bible lying there. It was turned to Song of Solomon. Tyler had solved the note on his cast.

Just yesterday she had recalled their moments on the couch as she readied herself for church. A telltale mark rested at the base of her neck, under her ear. She had done her best to cover it with a bandage and collared blouse, but it still burned, like a brand on her soul.

She rubbed her neck as a thought occurred to her. Had she prayed for Tyler? Really prayed for him? Not for his attention, not for his amazing kisses, not for a relationship to develop between them, but for him. For his heart. For his soul. That he would find the one thing that made him leave his family in Utah and move to a ranch in the middle of Texas, where he had searched for nine long years.

She watched them drive away and made up her mind to pray for him daily. The rest would be up to God.

# TWENTY-TWO

"SHORTCAKE?" Reggie's look was inquisitive as he helped Tyler into his truck.

Tyler shrugged. "She's short and sweet. It fits."

"How sweet was she?"

Tyler winced. "It wasn't like that. She was just helping me out."

Reggie backed out of the parking spot. "There were no sparks? No sizzle? No passion? She didn't make a move on you at all? Five weeks together, and nothing?"

"You sound like Mrs. Houston. I think she secretly hoped we were 'playing house,' as she called it. But it was strictly platonic." Except for those smokin' hot kisses.

Reggie grunted. Tyler knew he had seen the goodbye kiss, the looks between them, the tears building in Georgia's eyes. Oh, there was definitely a spark.

"We were all at the Blue Bull together, remember? You practically had steam coming out of your ears when I danced with her."

"I was not jealous." His denial was just a little too strong. "I was just wishing I could dance, that's all."

"Um-hm. And what was that on her neck today?"

Tyler looked sharply at Reggie, his eyebrows furrowed. There was something on her neck? He hadn't looked very closely at her the last couple of days. Thinking quickly, he made something up. "She switched detergents. She must be allergic to it."

"Did the detergent also leave that, um, bruise on her neck?" Reggie's eyes twinkled and he lifted his eyebrows knowingly. "Is that why you called me yesterday? Things get a little too close for comfort?"

"I don't know what you're talking about."

Tyler turned his face back to the window and stared at his reflection. This conversation had quickly become uncomfortable. But he had great respect for Georgia. He would not kiss and tell. Did he really leave a hickey on her neck? He hadn't noticed it. But he had avoided her since those rather intense moments together. Had others already seen it? Would more rumors spread? He couldn't leave fast enough.

Reggie chuckled and patted him lightly on his shoulder. "C'mon, lover boy. Let's get you back to the ranch. It's good to see you back in action."

•—————•

TYLER WATCHED out the window as they pulled into the ranch where he had spent nearly a decade moving cattle from one field to the next. This was home. The ranch hands were his family. But maybe it was no longer enough. His brain and heart had gotten too muddled once he realized how Georgia felt. And he knew he couldn't stay there anymore.

He didn't want anyone to have any other reason to talk about her.

He grabbed his duffle bag from the backseat of the ranch truck and hobbled into the bunkhouse, going to his room that had been empty since the accident. He tossed the bag onto the floor, then stretched out on the bed with his hat over his eyes. He knew the onslaught of "welcome backs" would begin as soon as the others came in from wherever they were working today. Right now, he just wanted some peace and quiet. His heart had tumbled when he saw Georgia's tears. But he wasn't sure whose heart was broken worse. Hers? Or his?

•·————··

GEORGIA PICKED up her phone and slumped onto the couch, dialing Ellen's number.

"Ellen, he's gone." Georgia couldn't hide the catch in her voice. "He just left. I don't think he was even going to say good-bye. He had everything packed, and Reggie was here to pick him up when I got home." Now the tears started flowing in earnest.

"Oh, honey. You knew he would." Ellen had been clear with Georgia from the beginning, reminding her to guard her heart. But when Georgia did anything, she was all in.

"I wasn't going to tell you this," Ellen stated. "But since Tyler is gone, I guess it won't hurt. In fact, it might help."

Georgia propped her feet up on the ottoman, mentally preparing herself for whatever bomb Ellen was about to drop. Lily curled up next to her feet, sniffing Tyler's leftover scent before lying down.

"Tell me what?" She reached for a tissue from a box by her side.

"Sam went to your apartment to talk to Tyler while we were in church yesterday."

Georgia switched her phone to her other ear. "Why would he do that? Did he tell Tyler to leave?"

"No. Tyler asked him to swing by, wanting to talk. I guess together they figured out what your message on his cast meant." Ellen got quiet, letting her words sink in. Baby babble from a distant room covered the silence.

"Oh. I found my Bible on the dining table, and it was opened to that verse. I kind of guessed he had solved the riddle. And then he ran. Just like that." Tears leaked from Georgia's eyes again.

"He told Sam he wasn't good enough for you. Sam told him he should talk to you about that. I'm guessing he didn't." Georgia heard footsteps, then what sounded like Ellen patting the baby's back as she spoke.

"No, he didn't. He must not feel the same way about me." But if that's true, why did he kiss me the way he did? Georgia kept that thought to herself.

"Do you want me to come over?"

"Would you? That might help."

They talked together for over an hour. Georgia told Ellen about some of the things they had done together, leaving out their scorching kisses from two days ago. Ellen listened without comment as Georgia talked through it all, and if she saw the small bruise on Georgia's neck, she didn't say anything. It wasn't the first time they had discussed Tyler, but it felt to Georgia like it might be the last.

Finally, her tears began to subside. But the damage to her heart was already done.

# TWENTY-THREE

TYLER WAS glad to be back in the saddle again. Cap snorted at him when he made the first trip to the barn, happy to see Tyler but a little miffed at having been ignored for so long. Tyler knew that his horse had been well cared for. Horses were critical to ranch operation, and each one of them received full care, but more than that, a horse was a cowboy's best friend. A lot of ranches have designated wranglers who care for all the horses. At the Double H that was also true, but each ranch hand always provided the daily care for their own animals. They were more than a tool for moving around the ranch. They were friends.

Tyler still had some aches in his injured extremities, but the orthopedic specialist told him he would probably experience that from time to time. Especially during bad weather. It made him think of his conversation with Georgia during the storm, which led to remembering the story they had created together. He wished he had asked for a copy of that.

He also sent what he hoped were appropriate thank-you gifts. The flowers were yellow roses mixed with daisies. The roses expressed gratitude, and she had said daisies were her favorite. He hoped she understood his meaning in the bouquet.

He also sent her a guitar from a local music store, and hoped she would take the time to learn to play it. He smiled as he remembered the way she played the piano without any music, making up a tune as her fingers tinkled the genuine ivory and ebony keys. She could surely do that with the guitar as well. Maybe someday he would see her playing at the Blue Bull. Wouldn't that make the rumors fly?

Cap greeted him at the stall door, and Tyler rubbed the white blaze on the horse's nose before walking through the small gate. Pulling an apple out of his pocket along with his knife, he cut the apple into pieces and fed them, one at a time, to the Quarter Horse. He owed Cap extra attention, even though his absence had not been a negligent act. The horse didn't know that. Tyler grabbed a curry comb and brush and began working through the animal's chestnut-colored coat, mane, and tail. He had missed this activity.

Grooming his horse was one of the most soothing things he did. The action not only helped bond with the horse, it gave him time to decompress and think about things other than ranching. Yeah, sometimes he thought through his to-do list, but today, his thoughts returned to the last few weeks and his time spent with Georgia.

The kisses they had shared on the couch that day had almost made him want to spill his heart to her right there. If he hadn't been so trussed up with casts on his leg and arm, he might have never let her go. But when the music changed to "I Heard it Through the Grapevine," he knew he had overstepped. Her life was that of teacher, singer, church. His was cowboy, ranch, and bars.

He pulled a hoof pick out of his hip pocket. Picking up a front leg, he ran his hand along the muscle from the knee down, feeling the joints and tendons for swelling. He then began the process of cleaning around the shoes, checking for wear and missing nails. He also cleaned around the frog, which is the soft tissue in the hoof that provides cushioning and traction. A healthy frog was critical to hoof care. Finally, he checked the hoof itself. Cap would need trimming soon, and he didn't think he could bend over long enough yet to do that. He would call the ranch farrier.

He repeated this process with the other legs, trying not to think about Georgia as he did. Cap stamped impatiently, even while having one foot suspended when Tyler worked on it. His horse had great balance. Overall, he was satisfied that the guys had taken good care of him while he was gone.

He saddled Cap, checking the blanket first for burrs or anything that would irritate him while he rode. Georgia was a burr that had gotten under his skin. He shook his head, clearing the thought.

He placed the saddle over the blanket and tightened the cinches, tapping Cap's side as he did to make the horse exhale. Cap had a habit of trying to keep his belly distended so that after the cinches were tightened, he could exhale and still have some breathing room. Unfortunately, that meant that the saddle might slip while riding, endangering the rider. Tyler knew all of Cap's tricks, however. He pulled the cinch tighter, and Cap turned his head to look at him.

"Gotcha boy, didn't I?" He patted Cap's rump.

Swinging into the saddle, he felt at peace. This was home. This was where God had meant him to be. Riding the range, pushing cattle around. Did Georgia have a place in that kind of a future? And where did the thought about God come from? She must have rubbed off on him. His lips turned up in a slow smile.

"What's the grin for? Thinking about the teacher?" Reggie had snuck up on him.

"Glad to be back in the saddle. I've missed this." Tyler would never admit he had been thinking about Georgia, but he knew Reggie had caught him daydreaming.

"Boss says to take it easy for a few days. It'll probably take a bit for you to get up to full strength, and we still need the doc to sign off that you are good to return to your full schedule."

"Yeah, but I need to get back at it. I'd much rather sit in a saddle than in that wheelchair."

Reggie and Tyler rode one of the near fence lines together, inspecting as they went. They found three places where the wire was down and worked together to make the repairs.

"You gonna see her again?"

Tyler had hoped Reggie wouldn't bring Georgia up. He should have known better.

"I don't know. Probably not. She's cute and all, but we are worlds apart. It wouldn't work."

"Didn't it work when you were staying with her? Or did y'all fight? Although making up would have been fun." Reggie tweaked a wire with his fence tool to tighten it before pounding the staple that held it to the wooden post.

"We actually got along pretty well. But she was at school most of the day, so I spent a lot of time just resting and watching videos. And the therapists came during the week, so they provided a large part of the assistance that I needed."

"And that was it, just like that? You don't want to see her again?"

"Let it rest, Reggie." Tyler was getting tired and grumpy. The sun was hot, his shoulder was hurting, and they needed to move on from this conversation. Reggie took the hint.

GEORGIA FLIPPED her phone over in her hand. She sat on the couch, in the very spot where he had kissed her so thoroughly, reliving those moments in her mind. She had reveled in his attention. And although she stiffened unintentionally when that next song began to play, she knew she was the one who had killed the moment. If she hadn't, where would it have led? Probably too far.

She hit the button for the story they recorded together, like she had done several times in the past weeks, and a tear slipped down her cheek. It turned into a rainstorm as she listened to his voice, remembering the way they had laughed together as they spun the story. She had not intended to lose her heart to the tall cowboy. In fact, several people had warned her to guard her heart.

In the corner of the room sat the beautiful guitar that Tyler sent to her. It was called a hummingbird because it had scrollwork on the pick guard that pictured a honeysuckle vine and a hummingbird within the vine. It was delivered one day out of the blue, a couple of weeks ago. She looked it up online and flinched when she saw what it was worth. He included a case, several picks in different styles, a tuner, extra strings, and a tutorial book. It was really a very thoughtful gift. The tone was clear and sweet, reverberating the melodies as she picked them with her fingers, but every time she played, she saw his gray eyes, and that made it difficult to focus on the notes.

She looked at the vase of yellow roses he had also sent to her. The daisies died, and she had picked them out of the arrangement. But the roses, which dried, still looked lovely in their own way and were sitting in the middle of the dining table. She was shocked he remembered that she said she liked daisies. But the roses were unexpected. They would never recover, never bloom again. They were stuck in time forever. Was she stuck in time? Would she move on? Could she?

She opened the music app on her phone, selecting the oldies playlist that had been playing when they had their moment on the sofa. It was still cued to where she had stopped it in the middle of falling to pieces, and flipped to the next song. Georgia groaned at Conway Twitty's velvety voice as he crooned "It's Only Make Believe."

"Okay, God. I get the message." She shouted to the empty room. "It was only make-believe. Temporary. A figment of my imagination. I have no one to blame but myself." The room refused to answer, allowing her mind to wander further.

"I really wanted him to care. But I don't know what I was thinking. I guess it was just a foolish dream. How could I fall in love with him?" She looked at her empty ring finger. Would it stay empty forever?

The heart wants what it wants. She had heard that expression many times, but was finally beginning to understand it. Lily even moped around, sniffing the spot on the couch where Tyler sat the most, or curling up on his bed. But once the cowboy figured out the message she had written on his cast, he bolted like a scared rabbit. Their time together hadn't been real to him. That much was obvious. But now he held a piece of her heart that she would never give to another man. It was his, alone. Did he even realize that? She put her hands over her face and cried.

Someone knocked on the door. Georgia rubbed the hem of her shirt over her face to make herself presentable, frowning when she realized she had smeared her makeup. Mrs. Carson and Mrs. Houston entered and immediately pulled her into a group hug.

"We heard you yelling through the walls. Are you okay,

dear?" They both talked at the same time, their hands patting her back from each side.

The song taunted her, and she shrugged loose so she could turn off the recording, which had continued to repeat in a loop. "Yes, I'm fine."

The duo of neighbors tsked. "That young man. Don't worry, dearie. He'll come around." Mrs. Carson's eyes held sympathy as she patted Georgia's hand.

Georgia shook her head.

"I saw the way he looked at you while he was here. He's in love with you, I'm sure of it." Mrs. Houston was adamant, her hand on Georgia's arm and her head nodding as if she had a crystal ball.

"Would you like company, dearie?" Mrs. Carson looked around like she was ready to settle in for the day.

"Or do you want us to go over to that ranch and yank him by the ear until he sees reason?" Mrs. Houston was always one to take the bull by the horns. Georgia chuckled at the mental image. At least it offered some comic relief.

"No, but thank you. To both suggestions. I think I just want to be alone. And I'm sorry if I disturbed you."

"Well, if you need anything, just yell. These walls are certainly thin enough."

The ladies left her in peace, but she still fidgeted. Dialing her phone, she called Ellen. It was time for some serious soul-searching.

# TWENTY-FOUR

GEORGIA HEADED SOUTH of town in her hybrid car. Her little green stink bug, as Tyler liked to call it. It had actually served her well over the past six years. She bought it used from an older lady who literally only drove to the grocery store and church, so it had low miles on it at the time. Now it was creeping up toward two hundred thousand miles, but they were miles well spent.

Her radio blared, playing music from her favorite satellite station. She sang along with the contemporary Christian music, rocking her head back and forth as she did. The GPS on her phone provided directions to her destination, calling out the turns as she drove. She had found a spot southwest of town that would provide a couple of days of peace and serenity. She needed the time to gather her thoughts about the past few weeks and where her life was going.

A sign flew by and she realized she had missed a turn, having tuned out the GPS in her head as she sang. Ugh. There were no crossovers or turnarounds on this stretch of highway. She would have to either turn around at the next exit, which was several miles away, or find a way to connect back to the road she should have turned on. Texas had a lot of farm roads and most were mapped. Plus, Georgia enjoyed a good adventure, often going sight-seeing to out-of-the-way places. Piece of cake.

She took the next exit and rather than turning around, drove about a mile before finding a small road that she thought would take her back to her original route. She turned onto that road, admiring the Hill Country scenery as she drove. The road got narrower and ended at another crossroad, which was nothing more than dirt.

She was about to go back when she spotted a grove of cottonwood trees. The temperature gauge on her car was rising with the heat. Maybe she should stop a bit, let her car cool down, then follow her path back to the main road.

Her car sputtered and died just as she made it to the grove of trees. Frustrated, she got out and lifted the hood. Steam rolled from the radiator. She was stuck.

She picked up her phone to dial for help and found no bars. No service? Where was she, anyway? She hadn't paid enough attention as she was driving because she was singing at the top of her lungs. She looked around for a house or other sign of a residence, but found nothing. Her eyes burned from the bright sun, so she shaded them with her hand. She was in a long valley with hills stretched up on either side. They were tall, and she didn't want to climb to the top since it would be a long, steep walk. Maybe it was better that she sit here for a while. She would check her phone periodically for service and hopefully get a call or at least a text message out to Ellen soon.

Fortunately, she had planned ahead and had a small cooler in her back seat with several bottles of water. She poured two bottles into the radiator, but she would have to save some of it for herself. When she turned the key in the ignition to crank the engine it coughed, then sputtered. She added another bottle and tried again. Knowing nothing about car engines, she kept trying until she was down to her last two bottles. She tried one more time, then heard nothing. Not even a click. Great. Her battery was dead, and now she couldn't even keep her phone charged. She was in trouble.

"God, help me, please. I'm lost. Please send someone to help me." It was a simple prayer, but she had faith that God would help her. Now to sit back and wait. She had no music, and no cell service. There were only the sounds of nature around her.

A soft breeze blew through the trees.

*"Be still and know that I am God."*

The words came to her as surely as the whisper of the wind. She sat quietly, taking in her surroundings. She was in a small grouping of trees, with the valley stretching out to either side, and the dirt road behind her. The day was hot. The sun beamed down through a cloudless sky.

She opened her car doors to allow the breeze to sweep through. A lizard ran under the car, making her jump. It was small and blue, but a reptile was a reptile, in her book. No need to invite trouble there. Scanning the ground, she didn't see any snakes. She had no idea which were venomous and which weren't, although she remembered something in her science class about a pointed nose versus a round nose. But which was which?

She should have brought a book to read. The paper kind she could hold in her hands that wouldn't require a battery. But all she had was a tablet, that she hadn't charged before she left, and had no way to charge it now, either.

Looking around, she took in her surroundings again. It was a beautiful valley, in its rugged way. But it also looked as abandoned as she felt.

Tyler had gone back to his life. She was happy that he had healed, but sad about what was apparently not to be. She was certain that God had brought them together. But she was wrong. And now she was stuck in the middle of nowhere, with no way to seek help except to pray. She was more alone than ever.

She had to have faith. That was it. God would protect her and send someone to find her. But as she looked around again, she wondered, "How?"

* * *

TYLER LOOKED up at the night sky from the tailgate of his brand-new truck. It was cloudy over Nora Hills tonight. There was no moon, no stars. Just airplanes flying lower than normal as they made their approach into San Antonio a hundred miles away, one every two minutes. He watched the green and red lights blinking on the tips of the wings, their glow bouncing off the clouds directly above them. Their front white landing lights flicked on as they made their approach. He could see them in the distance, lined up for miles off to the west. Tyler had always felt like he could see forever from this hill. But forever seemed like a long way off tonight.

The Fourth of July had come and gone, and he hadn't even gone into town for the parade and festival. Mr. Hudson hired a company to shoot fireworks over the lake for the guests staying at the ranch, so Tyler offered to make sure that the horses were secured for the night. He rode through the near pastures as well, talking softly to the cattle to keep them settled.

He told the bovines all about Georgia. About how he was drawn to her. The way she cared for her students, spending time to ensure that even the students who didn't really want to be in her class received the attention they deserved.

He told them about her bright smile. The way her eyes twinkled when she challenged him. The way she had shown a light on his heart, putting a spotlight on areas he had tried to bury. Illuminating the good and healing the bad. Forcing him to look to the future, and giving him hope.

Tonight, he felt like that light had gone out. He had a nagging urge in his chest, and he didn't know where it was coming from. So, he had taken his truck to the top of the hill to sit in the peaceful quiet. Maybe the answer would come to him that way.

Since returning to the ranch, he had spent the last few weeks healing physically. But he still felt bereft emotionally. He didn't like the party life anymore. He wasn't sure what had changed, only that he was no longer satisfied with anything. He had sent Georgia a thank-you bouquet of yellow roses and shared a couple GIFs with her, telling her how much he appreciated her support and help. But he was still not ready to make a commitment. He focused on healing his body. But he didn't know what to do about his heart or his soul.

He reached into a bag of snacks and water he brought along and pulled out the Bible that had been hiding unopened in the bottom of his locker at the bunkhouse since the day he moved there. His father had given it to him, along with the black hat, nine long years ago. To remind him that he had a family and a home. Tonight was the first time he had even picked it up since then.

Using the flashlight on his phone, Tyler ran his hands over the plush leather cover, noting its genuine feel. It still smelled new. New leather, new pages. He flipped through it with his thumb, the pages sticking together along the edges where they were embossed with gold. He flipped through it again to release those pages.

Wondering where to start, he searched for the verse that Georgia had written on his cast. SOS 8:7. Finding the table of contents, he followed his finger to the page number for Song of Solomon, then turned to that page, quickly finding chapter eight.

*"Many waters cannot quench love."* His part of Texas sometimes had dry spells. But when it rained, it was a flood. He didn't know if this was Georgia's way of telling Tyler that she loved him, or maybe that God loved him. Or maybe both.

Spying the ribbon bookmark, he turned further into the book, finding the New Testament and seeing the words printed in red. He remembered from his youth Sunday School class that the red letters meant the words had been spoken by Jesus. Then he noticed a big green circle drawn around one of the verses.

*"Greater love has no man than this, than to lay down his life for his friends."*

Georgia had shown him that love. She had sacrificed for him, even when the rumors called her all kinds of unpleasant names. She had shown him grace, even when he had gotten so horribly drunk that night. When he knew others were saying he wasn't good enough, she had shown him hope, that someone could love him for himself, after all.

He thought back to that first date by the lake. She looked so beautiful as she sat on the blanket, turning that leaf over and over in her hand. He had ruined it all, expecting more than he had a right to ask. Then she had been there when he needed her, anyway.

"Turn over a new leaf." The phrase that he had heard his grandmother say many times jumped out at him, the memory so strong he could almost see the kindness in her aquamarine eyes, hear the softness of her voice, and smell her famous cinnamon cookies baking in the oven.

Sitting up straight on the tailgate, he suddenly knew what he had to do. It had to be all or nothing, he could no longer straddle the fence. Pulling out his phone, he looked at the time. It was the middle of the night. Two a.m. here in Texas, one o'clock in Utah. But he took a deep breath and dialed a number that he had not dialed in far too long.

"Dad? It's Tyler."

GEORGIA LOOKED up at the night sky, reminded of the night she and Tyler had watched the moon together from the back of his truck and fallen asleep. There was no moon tonight and the valley was pitch black. She was thankful that the temperature had gotten cooler. Earlier today it was scorching hot, and she was out of water. If there was a creek nearby, she would have filled up her water bottles, but she didn't see anything within a short walking distance, and she didn't want to wander away too far. She knew she had to stay near her car in case somebody came by, which at this point did not seem likely.

An occasional plane flew over the quiet valley, providing the only light to her darkened world. She had been lost here for three days.

Nobody knew where she was. She told her sister she would call when she got where she was going, but hadn't even told her which direction she was taking. Another huge mistake, which she seemed to be making a lot of, lately.

There were no stars tonight, either, due to the cloud cover, but they couldn't help her anyway. Georgia had not studied astronomy and couldn't use them to navigate her way out of the valley. It would have been too dangerous to try because she didn't know the terrain. She could fall into a ditch and stay there until the buzzards found her. A shudder ripped through her. She knew what the huge birds did to dead animals they found on the roads. No, better to stay right where she was. She didn't want them circling over her body.

She tried singing, but her throat was scratchy from the lack of water. Even the crickets around her sounded better, their chirps blending together in harmony. She loved to sing with the birds that woke her up each morning, but she was sure that by tomorrow she would not even be able to whisper. She didn't have any tears left to cry, let alone sing.

Her skin was scratchy. Her sundress dirty. Her shoulders burned. Her eyes stung. Her hair felt like it had ants crawling through it. She had sweated a lot the first two days. Tonight, there was no sweat left.

*"Hey, God. I'm still here. You haven't sent anyone to help me yet. I'm not sure why. I prayed a prayer of faith. I've always trusted you. I sing for you every Sunday. And I've tried to follow your Word, even when it's hard."*

*"So why am I still here?"* The night was silent.

*"Hello? Are you there?"* Not even a cricket chirped.

*"Am I going to die?"* She would cry, but she had no tears left.

Would He send help? Why had God allowed this to happen? Wasn't He always supposed to provide a way out?

Did anybody even miss her? Here she was, nearing thirty, single, and oh, so very lonely. What would people say when they found her shriveled body? Her obituary would be short. Ellen was the only survivor to list. Three if you added Sam and the baby. If she ever got out of here alive. . . but no. That was not her bargain to make with God.

She ran her fingers over the gold cross she wore around her neck every day. There was nothing sentimental about it. She had purchased it at a discount jeweler when it was on sale. But it was a reminder to her of Whose she was. She was a child of God. She still didn't know why He hadn't rescued her. It was beginning to look like He wasn't going to. It could be years before anybody found her body here in the middle of an abandoned Texas valley.

Her vision began to blur as her body succumbed to the heat and lack of water. She closed her eyes and leaned back in the passenger seat, tilting it as far as it would go. It would be best to sleep, as long as she didn't dream about a certain cowboy in a beat-up black hat. Apparently, there was no future in that dream. That door had closed.

*"God, where are You?"*

# TWENTY-FIVE

TYLER SAT ON HIS BED, which once again hadn't been slept in. Boots stomped into the bunkhouse and straight to Tyler's room.

"Who did you have with you last night? Up on the hill." Tyler looked up, assuming his friend and coworker had seen the truck making its way up the ridge. Reggie's face held a curious expression.

"No one. I went up there to think." He stretched out on his bed and plunked his hat over his face.

Reggie walked further into the room. Tyler peeked through a hole in the hat. Reggie stood over him with crossed arms and spread legs.

"Leave me alone. I'm off, today."

"You didn't sleep here last night." Reggie's voice was sharp and reprimanding.

"I fell asleep in my truck."

"That's an old story. Try again."

What was it with Reggie this morning? He sounded more like his dad when he was a rebellious teenager. There were plenty of nights that his friend did not come back to the bunkhouse. He had no room to talk.

"Go away."

"Your teacher is missing." Reggie's huff blew through the hole in the hat.

Tyler tore his hat away and looked up into Reggie's face, only six inches away. His friend looked angry. And worried.

"My teacher?" Tyler furrowed his brow. "You mean Georgia?"

"Yeah," Reggie glared at Tyler, one eyebrow raised. "You know where she is?"

"No." He tried to put his hat back over his face, but Reggie snatched it away and tossed it to the side. Yep. There was that parental look. He will make a good father someday.

"I don't know where she is." Tyler speared his friend square in the face, lifting himself up on his elbows. "What's going on?"

Reggie adjusted his stance, leaning against the locker. "Well, apparently, she has disappeared, and the county rescue squad has asked for anybody who can, to help with the search. Boss wants us all to pitch in. The last time her cell phone hit a tower was four days ago and it's a pretty remote area with a lot of dead spots. They're planning to search by ATVs, horses, and air within a six-mile radius of the tower."

Tyler frowned and grabbed his hat. "Four days ago? She could be . . ."

Oh, dear God. He didn't want to think about the possibilities. "Why didn't you say that sooner? Let's go."

Tyler hopped out of Reggie's truck before he had even come to a stop in the parking lot where the search team was gathered. They had loaded up the horses in record time. Cookie had packed electrolyte drinks and snacks for the search crew.

He ran straight to Ellen and Sam. "I came as soon as I heard. What happened?"

Ellen sniffed back tears, her eyes red after having already cried several times that day.

"Georgia called and said she would be gone for a couple of days. That means two days, right? She said she would call again when she got where she was going. But she didn't tell me where that is. I haven't heard from her since." Ellen shuddered and looked up at Tyler, her face grim. "Do you know where she might have gone?"

"No, Ellen. I'm sorry. I haven't talked to her in a while. That was how long ago?"

"Four days."

Tyler listened as Ellen gave more details. Yesterday, she became worried and called the police. It took another day to get a court order to get her last known location from the phone company, which was a remote area on the edge of the Hill Country.

They had also confirmed with the airports and bus stations that she had not bought any tickets, nor was her car in any of those parking lots. She was not in any of the area hospitals, and her credit card records revealed no recent purchases, other than the gas she bought on her way out of town.

The Texas wilderness was vast. Finding her would be like looking for the age-old needle in the haystack.

Tyler turned and listened as the captain of the search team explained how the search would work.

"We'll start from the tower and work our way out. We have to cover over a hundred square miles and we will work in teams, so that nobody else will get lost. Drones will search from the air, but we will rely heavily on you guys." The captain nodded to the searchers. "Each team will have water with powdered electrolyte supplements, and a radio for communication back to base here at the tower. If you find her, radio immediately and we will send the evac helicopter to your location. It will be a hot, arduous search." The team captain took off his hat. "Let's pray together before we head out."

Tyler fidgeted his black hat in his hands as the captain prayed. He thought about the challenge ahead of them. Much of the Texas Hill Country terrain was rough, sandy, and full of cactus and scrub. If Georgia was lost out there, it would be difficult to find her.

•————•

GEORGIA SAT inside her car under the grove of cottonwood trees on the small dirt road she was on when her car sputtered and died. The shade helped protect her from the heat, but she had long since run out of the bottled water she had packed when she told Ellen she would be gone for a couple of days. School was out and she needed to get away and think, but now she had way too much time to think and no way to get home.

She had worn down the car battery by trying to crank the engine over and over. Then she couldn't charge her phone, which wasn't much good anyway because she was in a valley between two hills and had no cell service. And it could be miles to the next residence, the way ranches were scattered around here. She had always heard that if she was stranded, the best thing to do was to stay in one place and wait. But it had been four days, and she was hungry and thirsty. She no longer had the energy to try to walk out, even if she knew where to go.

She heard a low hum in the distance. If it was a helicopter, it was too far away to be looking for her. Or maybe she was hallucinating. Her vision swam again and the sound grew quiet.

She was grateful for the shade of the cottonwoods, but realized that with her small car under the grove of trees, it might never be seen from the air. Her open doors provided an avenue for the small breeze, and she prayed again. She prayed for her sister, who would mourn her, for the next person to rent her apartment, that they would find happiness, for her neighbors, that they would be blessed by the new renter, and finally for Tyler.

*"God, please take care of Tyler. If I never get to see him again, if I never get to tell him more about You, please look after him. He's lonely and hurting. And I love him so much."* She admitted it. She loved him. But it was too late.

She would probably die soon.

Georgia turned her head, trying to listen for the helicopter again. But her focus was fuzzy, and soon everything went black.

---

THE NATIONAL GUARD provided the air power. The ground team made up the foot power, using specially trained search and rescue dogs. They also had cadaver dogs, and Tyler hoped inwardly their sensitive noses would not find a body. Ellen had given them a piece of Georgia's clothing and her toothbrush to help the dogs find her scent.

Tyler chose to ride Cap, thinking it would be easier to scan the landscape from the elevated position. He could also get into places that an ATV couldn't go. Reggie rode along on his own horse, supplying additional eyes for scanning the terrain, and support for Tyler.

The teams worked in sectors, spreading out as they searched. Sometimes they rode shoulder to shoulder to make sure they wouldn't inadvertently walk around her. As they scoured through sand and scrub, Tyler recalled the past few months and the circumstances that had brought them together. The lake. The fair. The moon. The accident. The SOS. Would they find her? He sure felt like he had a huge hole in his heart right now.

The sun beat down in typical Texas-in-July ferocity, the temperature over the hundred-degree mark, and the heat index even higher. They came to a steep ravine and searched up and down the wide crevice before finding a place to cross. Every tree was investigated. Every place for a small car, or a body, to hide. Using binoculars, they scanned the horizon. They watched the sky for circling vultures. The sun burned into their eyes. And every time they thought they might have found her, the site turned up blank.

They found an abandoned, rusted-out truck. Remains of a deer carcass had been stripped clean by the buzzards. Armadillos and rabbits scurried under the brush. But there was no sign of Georgia.

Tyler adjusted his hat, wiping the sweat from his brow with his sleeve for the umpteenth time that day. He took a swig of water from his canteen.

"What are you thinking, Tyler?" Reggie also wiped his brow. Sweaty foam stained the horses' coats. They had been searching nearly eight hours and would lose daylight when the sun slid behind the western hills. They would have to turn back soon.

"We can't stop now. If we are this hot, imagine how bad Georgia must be. Especially if she has been out here for days. She could be injured. Lying in a ravine. Bitten by a rattlesnake. Hungry. Thirsty. Scared." He didn't want to express his worst fear. If she had no water . . .

Reggie nodded, allowing Tyler to think in silence. They crested a hill, scanning the valley below. They were near the fringe edge of the search area by this time and would have to regroup soon. The horses were also tired and needed water. A dead horse wouldn't help them at all.

Tyler's heart was breaking into pieces. He missed his Shortcake. Would he ever see her again? Not knowing what else to do, Tyler prayed inwardly as he scanned the landscape. *"God, I know I haven't exactly been friendly to you. Heck, I've run from you and from my family. I don't deserve anything. But God, please let us find Georgia. Not for me. But for her. Please let us find her alive."*

"What is that under those trees?" They were on a high ridge. Reggie squinted his eyes and pointed to a grove down in the valley.

Tyler picked up his binoculars to see more clearly since it was a good half mile from where they stood. His heart lurched, bile rising to his throat.

*Please God, let it be her.* The prayer was quiet on his lips, but a banging gong in his heart.

"It looks like a car, but I don't see anyone. Might be her tiny little hybrid. It's a weird color. She calls it olive green, and it would blend into the surroundings." Tyler radioed their location back to the search captain and advised they were going to check it out. The captain ordered air support to head that way.

•————•

GEORGIA WAS HOT, dizzy, tired, and afraid. Her legs cramped, the pain seizing the muscles. If she didn't get help soon, it would not go well for her. She would die out here, waiting for someone to find her.

A horse whinnied. Or was she dreaming? She had laid her seat back to rest and tried to get up, but nausea and dizziness took over. She heard shouting, which hurt her head. Felt a new breeze and smelled a familiar scent. Then she looked up through her heavy lids into gray eyes under a black hat, and knew she was dreaming. The image swam before her and the feeling of callused fingers roamed over her dry face.

Then she was floating, a gravelly voice pulling her into the whirlwind with low, soothing words. Was this what it was like to die? She felt strangely peaceful.

"I'm here, Shortcake. I've got you. Stay with me, please. I need you." The voice was soft and full of emotion.

She tried to speak, but nothing came out. She couldn't even lift her hand.

"Sh-h-h. It's okay. You're safe." Where had she heard that voice before? She felt herself being lifted into strong arms. Was she floating on a cloud, or hovering between life and death? Were the angels finally carrying her away?

The arms laid her on something soft and cushioned. Georgia felt a sharp stab in her arm and moaned. A cool sensation flowed through her veins to her chest, spreading through her torso, down her other arm, and all the way to her toes and fingers.

Her brain hurt. She heard numbers passed around over her head and tried to make sense of them. Did Heaven have a math class? Then she was floating again. More voices. More numbers. And shouting. Bright colors swirled behind her eyelids before disappearing into darkness. Then a distinct thump, thump, thump surrounded her. Angel wings? She wanted to see them. She wanted to see their glorious faces. Would they have gray eyes?

# TWENTY-SIX

TYLER WALKED into the waiting room of the emergency department at the same hospital where he had been taken less than four months ago. But now it seemed like a lifetime. Tears had leaked from his eyes as the helicopter lifted off the ground. He would gladly give her those tears and more if it would save her life. Georgia had been so hot and dry in his arms. Her skin crackled. Her lips were chapped and bleeding, her face and shoulders crimson, blistered, and peeling from days in the sun. He wondered how long ago she had stopped sweating, and hoped they weren't too late. He had pulled his phone out of his pocket to call Sam as soon as the helicopter lifted off, and found no service. Georgia, his beautiful Georgia, was truly stranded.

His eyes scanned the waiting room and the people who were also waiting for word on their loved ones. Some were looking at their phones. Some flipped mindlessly through any of the old magazines they kept there, some were asleep in twisted positions that would rival complicated yoga poses in the uncomfortable chairs.

He found Ellen and Sam in a corner. Sam held his arm

around Ellen while she sat, looking numbly at the carpet pattern on the floor. He caught Sam's eye and strode to where they huddled.

"Any word?" Tyler had a lot of time to think as he had returned via ATV from where they had found Georgia. He had taken a quick shower, and made the ninety-minute journey to the hospital. The search crew brought in a trailer for the horses, and Reggie took care of Cap for him.

"She's in room nine." Sam stopped and took a deep breath. "They won't let us go back, but the nurse that took our information said that it was lucky you found her when you did." Sam tilted his head and searched Tyler's eyes. "I think it was more than luck. I think God sent you to her."

Tyler swallowed and nodded in acknowledgment, taking the seat next to Sam. He leaned forward with his arms on his thighs. "I've been wondering the same thing. I prayed right before we found her, and then there she was. I just hope we weren't too late."

He knew room nine far too well, having been taken there after his accident. It was where they took the most critical patients, and a flood of memories hit him. The pain. The pokes, prods, and stabs. The smell of antiseptics and blood. The bright lights and dim voices. The constant beeps of the monitors. Images swirled and blurred around him as he relived his time in that room. And now, Georgia was in that same room, fighting for her life.

Ellen raised her head to look at Tyler, her eyes bloodshot and glassy, her skin puffy. She held her hand out and touched his arm. "I want to thank you, Tyler. I haven't been very nice to you. I hope you will forgive me."

Tyler shook his head slowly. "I haven't been very likeable. But Georgia is a remarkable woman. She has brought out things in me I hadn't thought possible in a very long time."

The trio looked up as a doctor entered the room through the double doors and approached them with something in his hand. He looked at Sam and Ellen.

"Mr. and Mrs. Skaggs, Georgia is one very fortunate woman. We are pumping fluids and treating her sunburn, which is pretty severe. We also ran an MRI and don't see any damage to the brain, heart, or kidneys, so we are hopeful. She has a very serious case of heatstroke, but I think you found her just in time.

The doctor held out the necklace that Georgia wore every day. "She told me to ask you to give this to somebody named Tyler."

"Doctor, this is Tyler." Ellen nodded her head, indicating him.

The doctor looked at him and smiled. "I see now why she asked me that question."

"What question was that?" He held out his hand, and the doctor gently placed a necklace into it before looking up at him again.

"She asked me if angels have gray eyes."

The small gold cross was so delicate and dainty against his roughened work-worn skin. Gold against calluses. Smooth against rough. Grace against sin. A refiner's fire made perfect. Tyler blinked back a tear.

"When can we see her?" Sam's question brought Tyler back to the moment.

"We are going to get her into a room first. I'd say it will be another hour or so, maybe two. Do you folks need anything?" The doctor looked between the three of them as they shook their heads.

"There is a cafeteria in the hospital. Just ask anyone at the desk and they can tell you how to get there." The doctor watched for their acknowledgment then walked back through the double doors.

Tyler broke into tears, collapsing into the chair nearest him. Georgia would be okay. Ellen sat in the chair next to him and wrapped her arms around him, crying with him. Sam placed his hands on both their shoulders. Tyler had never cried like this. But maybe it was about time. They sobbed softly together.

A few minutes later, Tyler sat up with a new resolve. Life was not guaranteed to any of them. He hadn't learned that lesson after his accident. But he learned it today. And he had a new goal. He had a woman to win.

———

SAM, Ellen, and Tyler all sat in Georgia's room, watching her as she slept. She was sedated, but occasionally her forehead would wrinkle as if she were thinking about something. They were all concerned for the woman they loved, and Tyler had to admit that yes, he loved her. There would be no more beating around the bush. He would court her with the respect that she deserved. Because he knew, without a doubt, that he really wanted to be the right guy for her.

He watched the numbers on her monitor. She had done the same for him not that long ago. He heard the clicks, the buzz, and the beeps. He watched the steady stream of drips from the intravenous bags. The doctor said she was severely dehydrated. Taking one of her hands in his, he kissed the back of her fingers and bowed his head to say a quick prayer, hoping that God was listening.

Lifting his head, Tyler focused on Ellen. "Is there anyone else who needs to be informed that Georgia is in the hospital?

Parents? Other family?" Tyler wondered about her family, since they had discussed his, but not hers.

"No, we have no one else to call. Our parents died thirteen years ago in a car accident. We don't have anyone else."

"I'm sorry. I didn't know that. That must have been a struggle for you. You both would have been pretty young."

"I was barely nineteen, Georgia had just turned sixteen."

"So you acted as her parent for a while. That must have been hard." Tyler was getting a new perspective on Georgia, and on Ellen.

"Yes, that's why it is so hard for me to give up and let her do her own thing, even now. I'm sorry I was so hard on you." Ellen drew in a ragged breath. Sam covered her hand with his in comfort.

"Tell me about her." Tyler nodded toward the bed. "What was she like as a little girl?"

Ellen chuckled. "Georgia was a whirlwind. Always happy, always on the go, always taking on whatever challenge came her way. Her mind raced at a hundred miles a minute. But she never caused any trouble. I think she was more of an adult than I was when our parents died."

Tyler could see that. There was a sense of responsibility in her that went beyond her normal daily duties. She had helped him more than once, even though doing so put her own reputation at risk. Rumors about her, about them, had flown through the town. They weren't true, but it didn't stop the gossip.

Her kisses had been sweet. And there was a passion there that he now realized drove everything she did. She did it all with gusto. He smiled at the memories.

Ellen breathed again. "There was a time when she found an injured squirrel. It was just a baby. She nursed it to health, even though our parents were afraid it might be rabid. When it started running around the house, our parents told her it was time to let it go. She cried for a week."

Yes, Tyler could see that scene in his mind.

He thought of her cat, Lily. Was she alone in the apartment? Did she have food? He made a mental note to stop by and let her neighbors know she was in the hospital, and check on the feline.

"She also had a heart for anyone younger than she was. She helped in the church nursery, and got on the floor with the kids to play their games right along with them."

"Where did you grow up?"

"That was up in Abilene. I met Sam in college, and we all moved here when Sam and I got married and he got the job with the private plane service."

Ah. So that was how they ended up in Nora Hills. Sam had a contract with the Double H, and other ranches. Quite a different story from his, since Georgia didn't leave home in rebellion like he had.

Tyler looked Ellen and Sam in the eye. "Look. I know the last few months have been. . . strange. Georgia and I seem to be as different as night and day. But she does something to me." He tapped his fist over his heart. "Makes me feel things I thought I would never feel." He took a breath, organizing his thoughts.

"She makes me want more out of life. More than just a good time. More than what people have said about me. I want a home. A family. I want love, and fidelity, and stability. The whole picket fence thing." He took a deep breath and shook his head, surprised at what he was finally admitting.

"I intend to do right by Georgia, with your approval. But it will take time. I have some things in my own life I need to clean up first." He meant every word, and they seemed to sense that. Ellen nodded and smiled. Sam nodded with her. He had won them over. Now to win over Georgia.

· ——————— ·

GEORGIA STIRRED AND MOANED. "Where am I?"

All eyes turned to her. Her throat was dry and scratchy, which was to be expected, and it sounded painful. Her eyes drooped as she spoke.

"Where are the angels? I want to see the angels."

Ellen was immediately at Georgia's side. "What angels, sweetie?"

"They picked me up, and I floated with them. It was so beautiful. I could hear the fluttering of their wings. And they had gray eyes that glowed."

"You are in the hospital, Georgia. You were flown here in a helicopter. That must be the angels you are thinking of."

"Hospital? What happened?"

"You decided to take a detour down a dirt road and got lost. What in Heaven's name made you do that?"

Georgia scrunched her face, her thoughts now coming more clearly. "I. . . I missed a turnoff. I think. I tried to take a shortcut back to the exit." She rubbed her forehead.

"My head hurts."

"I'll call the doctor." Ellen pushed the nurse call button.

"That's right. I was lost. And my car died. And I didn't have cell service. Or water. How did you find me?" She coughed again. Her throat was still scratchy.

"Tyler found you."

The nurse came in, added another bag to her IV drip, and sat a cup of ice chips on the bedside table, then left.

Tyler stepped into her field of vision, over Ellen's shoulder.

Ellen stepped away, allowing him to take the chair next to the bed, and he took her hand, cradling it gently to avoid the IV they had placed there. She was so dehydrated, the nurses had a hard time finding a vein that would work. They had poked her in several different places, leaving bruises at each site.

She locked her eyes on his. Those were the gray eyes she remembered. Was he her angel? The love she saw there made her shiver. Tyler quickly adjusted her blanket, but Georgia shook her head. She pushed it back and set her hand on top of it, her fingers linking with his. The pair sat that way for several minutes. Georgia let her eyes close and Tyler gently rubbed his thumb back and forth across her fingers. It was one place she did not have peeling blisters from her sunburns.

Jerking awake, she searched for those gray eyes again. Her brain was still foggy.

"You found me."

"We searched for eight hours." Tyler picked up the cup. "Here. You want some ice chips?"

"No. I just want you." Peace finally came over her, her words fading from her lips as her eyes closed and she slipped into a restful sleep.

Georgia woke up later to find Tyler sitting in a chair near the foot of her bed. The nurse had come in to draw blood. Seven vials. They had to use the back of her other hand because her veins were so depleted from being dehydrated. She felt something rubbing her foot and realized that he had his boot off and was rubbing his foot against hers, his eyes intense. It was enough of a distraction that she was able to block out the pain of the blood being drawn. Then she saw a flash of gold around Tyler's neck.

"You're wearing my cross."

TYLER HAD GONE to the small gift shop on the first floor of the hospital and found a longer chain, hanging her cross on it so it would fit around his neck. He lifted his hand to pull it up where she could see it, waiting while the nurse finished.

Once the nurse had her blood and left the room, he put his foot back into his boot and moved the chair to where it had originally been, near her head. He picked up her hand and turned it palm up, tracing the lines there with his finger. He circled her thumbprint, then pressed his thumb to hers.

"You know, Georgia, I don't know what I would have done if we hadn't been able to find you. You scared all of us. You scared me." Tyler's eyes turned a darker shade of gray. He wouldn't even try to hide what he was feeling right now. Gratitude to God that they had found her. Gratitude that she would heal. And gratitude for the love that she had shown him.

"When this is all over, I have plans for us. I can't tell you what they are right now, I'm still working out the details. And there are some things I need to do with myself, too. But first, we need to get you well." He continued to stroke her fingers with his.

"I'm half tempted to offer to stay with you. To take care of you the way you took care of me. But Sam would probably skin me alive." He shook his head at how he and Sam had bonded over the last couple of days.

"So once you are out of here, you are going to stay with your sister for a while. Until you are back on your feet. I'll visit as much as I can. And in the meantime, well. . . I can't tell you what I'm working on in the meantime. But I promise you will like it. I hope."

Tyler was true to his word. He spent most of the three days

that Georgia was in the hospital by her side. And when she was released and moved to Ellen's house, he was there as often as he could possibly be. He brought Lily to her from her apartment, carrying the cat carrier in one arm, and the enclosed litter box in the other. He even shook fingers with Sam Jr. The little tyke had grown on him.

The other ranch hands filled in for him once again, and even Ritz pitched in to help. Reggie was stepping up to the plate, too. Tyler could see a change in him lately. This summer had affected them all with first Tyler's accident, then Georgia getting lost. It was as if the world had tilted further on its axis. Life was changing for all of them.

# TWENTY-SEVEN

"IS THIS SEAT TAKEN?"

Tyler stood in the aisle, next to the pew where Georgia sat with Ellen and Sam. She had recovered from her heatstroke, and it was her first Sunday back in church. They all scooted over to make room for him and he sat down next to Georgia, on the end.

He drummed his fingers on his leg during the song service. He and Sam had talked quite a bit since Georgia's incident, and Tyler had shared his plans with Sam, receiving his approval. Today was step two. He had already implemented step one by calling his father again. Georgia placed her hand on top of his. The drumming stopped, but then Tyler began to tap his heel silently. He was restless, and he knew everyone in his pew could feel it as their eyes turned his way.

"Nervous about something?" Georgia raised an eyebrow at him. He stopped tapping his heel.

The sermon was about the Shepherd who left his flock to look for the one that was lost. Tyler smiled inwardly. Yeah, he was the lost sheep. But Georgia had found him. Had seen value in him. And had shown him the unconditional love he had been craving for the past nine years. As the minister closed in prayer, Tyler prayed for acceptance. He felt more at peace than he had ever felt in his life. It was time.

The closing song was "Just As I Am." Tyler stood, handing his hat to Georgia, and she gaped up at him. He hadn't told her his plan. He had to work this out on his own, just between himself and God. He walked to the front of the church, shook the minister's hand, and waited for the song to conclude.

The last time he stood in front of this church, he was angry. The people here had treated him and Georgia unfairly. Well, mostly Georgia. Today, he felt like a new man with a new mission.

The minister introduced him again, and all eyes turned to him as he cleared his throat before speaking.

"I would just like to say that this year has been a year of challenges and changes for me. I met a beautiful young lady that I was very rude to in the beginning, and she and all of you let me know it." Everyone chuckled.

"Several months ago, I stood here, and I was angry with you. And with God." He glanced over at her before turning back to the congregation. "But Georgia showed me something about myself that I had not been willing to see up until now. That God loves me. She showed me His grace, just by being herself and accepting my apologies without asking anything in return. She showed me His peace through her calm compassion." Then he looked straight at Georgia. "And I want that peace, too."

Georgia smiled at Tyler, her eyes glistening. She nodded at him and waited for him to finish.

"She showed me Jesus. And I want what she has. So I would like to be baptized. Today. Here. Now. I don't want to wait another minute. I want to thank Jesus for loving this broken cowboy."

Georgia jumped from her seat and ran to Tyler, hugging him while others surrounded him. Someone went to the back closet and pulled out a couple of towels. They walked as an entourage to the river, which flowed behind the church in a slow, easy, stream. The sky was a brilliant blue, not a cloud to be seen anywhere. The temperature had even cooperated, holding in the upper eighties. Perfect for a dip in the river.

It took two men, Sam on one side, the minister on the other, while Georgia held his hat and his phone. He hadn't brought any other clothes so he was baptized in the same Wrangler jeans and plaid shirt he wore to church. Georgia met him with the towels as he came up out of the river, hugging him tightly. He kissed her right there in front of everybody, and they both ended up wet. Laughing together. He was surrounded again, people slapping him on the back or shaking his hand. He could not stop smiling. Miracles do happen, and he was proof.

⸱⸻⸱

TYLER AND GEORGIA sat next to the lake on their weekly picnic. It had been a little over a month since she had been released by the doctor. July had turned into late August, and the sun had grown even hotter, but the breeze off the lake was pleasant. It was the only kind of date that Tyler would offer. He figured it was safe, and Georgia deserved safe.

School would start soon. Georgia was looking forward to getting back to her students, but she had a restlessness that would not be satisfied. She needed to know where she and Tyler stood.

"Tyler, what are we doing?" He still wore her cross around his neck.

"Hm? We're laying on a blanket, enjoying the breeze off the lake. It's a nice breeze today, too." The voice came from under his beat-up black hat, which he wore over his face.

Georgia rolled over and faced him, pulling his hat aside. "That's not what I mean, and you know it." She placed her hand on his chest. Possessively, this time.

Tyler placed his hand on hers and turned it over in his. Kissing her fingers.

"Tyler, kiss me." She pointed to her mouth, but her eyes said much more than the simple statement. Tyler drew in a breath, then gently rolled her over, capturing her hands. He looked at her mouth all healed and soft again. It would be so easy. He refocused his gaze from her mouth to her ponytail, pulled on the scrunchie that she had used to tie it up, and spread her silky auburn tresses across her shoulders. His eyes were cloudy with indecision, remembering their first date here. He was a different man now, and they both knew it.

"Georgia, if I kiss you now, I won't want to stop. And I won't do that to you again. You will have to be patient with me." His gray eyes twinkled, as if they held a secret.

"What are you waiting for? Why do I have to be patient?"

He rolled away from her onto his back, looking through the tree above them at the sky. "I can't make a commitment to you yet. And I won't kiss you silly until I can."

"What if I want you to kiss me silly?" Georgia rolled on her side to look at him again, then frowned.

"Wait. What are you not telling me?" She tried to pull away, but he stopped her with his hand on her arm.

Tyler kissed her on her forehead, as he had each week. "I can't tell you everything yet. And I know that is driving you crazy.

But you don't have to be worried." Her brow was furrowed. "I promise. I just want to be worthy of you, Georgia. And that means you need to give me time to finish what I'm working on. Until then, I'm asking you to trust me." He stood, holding his hand out to help her up. "Come on. It's time to take you home."

＊————————＊

THE FOLLOWING WEEK, Tyler picked Georgia up at their usual time and headed out of town. But this time, he took the highway southwest, away from the Double H and toward the South Fork of the Guadalupe. They drove for about twenty minutes before Georgia realized they had taken a different path.

"Where are we going?" Georgia looked at Tyler from behind her sunglasses.

Tyler reached across the console and took her hand. "It's a surprise."

In another half hour, Tyler turned onto a dirt road that looked vaguely familiar to Georgia. Then her eyes widened. They pulled up under the grove of cottonwood trees where she had been stranded for four days, and where Tyler had found her. "Why are we here?"

Tyler opened his door and got out of the truck, then came around to Georgia's side and opened the door for her. He had ordered the truck specifically to include electronic steps that slid into position when the door was opened. Taking her hand, he helped her out of the cab and closed the door, then guided her to the back of the truck. He took her by the waist and lifted her to the open tailgate, hopping up beside her.

"You remember this place, right?"

Georgia nodded. "I was so lost. My car died, my cell phone died, and I didn't have service anyway, then I ran out of water."

"Do you know how scared I was that day we were looking for you? Thinking how remote it is out here and how we might never find you?" Tyler looked ahead at the grass that was waving along the sides of the dirt road.

Georgia listened in silence. She understood that Tyler had more to say and was trying to determine how to say it. She waited for him to gather his words together.

He looked up toward the high hillside. "The night before I found out you were missing, I was up on the hill on the ranch, our pink moon hill, thinking. By myself." He looked over at her. "I haven't seen anyone else since meeting you."

Turning back to face the road, he leaned forward on the tailgate, his hands pressed to the metal on either side of him for balance. "I called my father." Georgia raised her eyebrows but didn't say anything. "In the middle of the night. And we talked for nearly two hours."

"You called your father?" Georgia was surprised.

"I told him all about you. How you had showed me things about myself that I never would have realized otherwise. I told him about my accident, and about how you took care of me afterwards. I said you were beautiful, and charming, and teasing, and soft, and sweet. And that I never want to live without you."

He turned to her, drawing her eyes to his, one hand cupped around her face. "Because I am hopelessly and completely in love with you. You finish me. You are the other half that I have been missing for a very long time." He turned back toward the road again. "You know what he said? He said, 'Well then son, go and get her'." Tyler was silent again for a moment, drawing a breath, composing his next words. Georgia continued to wait.

"But then Reggie told me you were missing. We searched

for hours over what seemed like impossible terrain. I thought I had lost you forever. It scared me so much, what you might be going through. That you might have fallen into a ravine with a twisted leg. Or been bitten by a snake. Or your car was upside down, like my truck was, and you had been hanging that way for days. I had so many bad possibilities going through my mind. But the worst thought was that I might never see you again."

He wrapped his arms around her, pulling her close, tucking her into his side.

"I looked down from that ridge up there," Tyler pointed to the top of the hill directly in front of them. "I asked God to tell me where you were. And we found you here. Well, Reggie saw your car first. But I knew it was you."

Georgia reached out to touch Tyler's leg, just above his knee. It was a light touch, but they both felt the emotion behind it. He was in love with her. She had to absorb this new thought because she had been in love with him for months.

"I took a trip to think. I was cruising along, minding my own business, singing loudly. I missed my turn. Then, of course, I got lost. I'm not sure how I got so far off the beaten path. I think I was just looking for complete solitude. I knew I had fallen hard for you, and I didn't know what to do about it. Especially since you hadn't called me after you went back to the ranch." Georgia drew hearts on his leg with her finger.

Tyler stood up and took Georgia's hands to help her down off the tailgate. "Let's walk a bit. I want to show you something." He continued to hold her hand, pointing around the valley with his other hand, showing her landmarks as he spoke. "This ranch spreads out over ten thousand acres up and down this valley. It has been abandoned for several years. The owners decided they didn't like Texas heat and moved back to Wyoming. But for some reason they kept ownership. Paid the taxes on it and everything, even though they didn't live here. Yesterday, my father and I closed on it."

"You bought it?" Georgia looked around, surprise in her voice. It was a beautiful place, in spite of the memories of being lost.

"Yes, we pooled our money and created a corporation. We bought the land and intend to restore it to a proper ranch. It will be a great place to raise cattle, and the market is good right now. We are calling it the Thousand Hills Ranch."

"Thousand Hills?"

"Yes, from Psalms 50." He pulled a screenshot up on his phone.

*"I bring no charges against you concerning your sacrifices*
*or concerning your burnt offerings, which are ever before me.*

*I have no need of a bull from your stall*
*or of goats from your pens,*
*for every animal of the forest is mine,*
*and the cattle on a thousand hills."*

"That's beautiful. I've never read those verses before."

"Ah. I finally taught you something new, teacher." His grin shone brighter than the gorgeous sunshine, illuminating the love in her soul.

He pointed across the valley to a spot facing southwest. It was an open field, slightly elevated up the hill, a lake at the bottom, and trees on the backside, with a clear view of the valley and the setting sun.

"That's where I want to build our home. I figure it will also be a great place to raise kids. Our kids." He looked back at Georgia, hope in his eyes.

She faced him and put her hand on his chest.

"Tyler, I have been in love with you ever since that day you showed up at church to defend my honor. I couldn't believe you did that. It told me that everything everyone said about you was wrong."

She took a break, composing her thoughts.

"When I saw your truck upside down in that ditch, my heart jumped into my throat. And I thought we had really grown into something more than just friends while you stayed with me. Then you left and just kind of disappeared. I didn't know what I had done but whatever it was, it was probably too much. I thought I had scared you away with the SOS."

"Your SOS saved me. I might have never found God's grace without it. But I knew I wasn't ready for you yet. I've been spending the last few weeks searching."

"Have you found what you are looking for?" Georgia studied his eyes, trying to discern his meaning.

•———————•

TYLER LOOKED OVER HER HEAD, then back to her eyes. He searched for confirmation of what he hoped was true. Even though she had said the words, he needed to see it in her face. And he found it there, somewhere between her lips, her dimple, and those brilliant emerald eyes.

Nodding his head because he couldn't trust his mouth to speak without a squeak, he pulled her closer.

"Last week you said you couldn't kiss me silly yet. Can you kiss me silly now? Because I would really like you to kiss me." Her mouth turned up in her sweetest smile, her head tilted, eyebrow raised.

Tyler placed his hands loosely behind her back. He roamed his eyes over her face, down to her lips, ready for kissing. He moved his gaze back to her eyes. Those green gems made him melt every time he looked into them. He loved the beautiful dimple in her left cheek. The way she made his heart beat like a syncopated clock. He drew another breath in and let it out slowly.

"The only woman I ever want to kiss silly, from this day forward, is my wife. Or at least, my soon-to-be wife. But she has to be able to solve this puzzle first." He pulled a green velvet box out of his pocket and opened it to reveal a spectacular emerald ring. The large center stone was flanked by small diamonds on each side. He took the ring out of the box and tilted it for Georgia to look at closer. "Read the inscription on the inside." He held his breath, waiting.

"It says 'SOS 3:4'" Georgia grinned. "That will be easy to solve." She pulled out her phone to look it up, only to realize she didn't have service.

"Ugh! You did this on purpose!"

Tyler chuckled. He wrapped his arms around her tightly. He never wanted to let her go. "It says, *I have found the one whom my soul loves.*' What do you say? Will you be the one whom my soul loves, for the next, oh, maybe hundred years? Or however long God gives us together?" His eyes lit up as he waited for her answer.

"Yes! For at least a hundred years. Forever. Or longer." Her eyes sparkled brighter than the ring as he slid it onto her finger.

He kissed her silly. His mouth found hers, softly at first, but quickly turning hungry to express what words couldn't say. He pulled the band out of her ponytail, releasing her crown of hair around their faces. Cupping her head with his hand, his fingers tangled in her hair, as her arms wrapped tightly around his neck. It was the culmination of waiting colliding with passion. He loved her. Heart, soul, body, and mind. He couldn't breathe without her. Couldn't exist without her. Would never be the same because of her. They moved together as a symphony. Him tasting her. Her tasting him.

Knees weak with passion, they dropped to the ground, their ground, and he drew her into his lap. They kissed until they were both breathless, fire burning through his gut. The slow burn continued to crawl through him.

"Fire ants!" He shot off the ground, dumping Georgia as he did. But she began beating on her legs, and he drew her up quickly. Together, they knocked the pesky bugs off each other, laughing as they danced away from the ant hill.

Finally free of the biting critters, he took her hands and stared into her eyes.

"I love you, Georgia Nicole Duncan."

"I love you too, Tyler Boseman Harriman Grant." Her green eyes twinkled like the ring he had just placed on her finger.

His heart squeezed as he hugged her against him, pulling her head to his chest. He smiled at how just a few short months ago he thought of her as just another date. How he had grown. He wanted to cherish the woman in his arms, and make her feel like the princess he thought her to be. Special. Precious in his eyes and God's eyes. A treasure to never be taken lightly.

He felt so free. He hadn't felt this way since he was baptized last month.

Georgia reached up and kissed him again. Just a quick peck, but one that sealed their love. They laughed together like kids on a playground.

"Come on." Tyler took Georgia's hand and led her back to his truck. "Let's go share our good news with your sister and her crazy husband. And maybe Mrs. Carson and Mrs. Houston."

# EPILOGUE

THEY TRADED her green stink bug for an SUV. It was sturdier, more reliable, and definitely more suited to ranch life. And Tyler actually fit in the SUV. She thought about the night he had folded up into the small hybrid and chuckled. Thankfully, those days were behind them.

Georgia loved driving down the road with the sunroof and windows wide open. She hadn't had one in her little car. She also marveled at the available options. It was more like flying a plane than driving a car. There was so much automation, she almost didn't have to drive at all. Maybe she would get Sam to help her get her pilot's license. She pictured herself with Tyler, flying over their new ranch. Wouldn't that be fun?

The commute to school would be much longer, but if they started a family, she would give that up. The thought made her blush. She was looking forward to their wedding in a way that made her cheeks turn red, imagining what their first night would be like. He was such a hunk, and he would be her hunk.

Georgia pulled down the dirt road. Tyler was already there, waiting for her. He had started building a driveway to the site where they would build their house. But first, they would put in a modular home, dig a well for water, install a septic system, add an LP gas tank, and a personal wind turbine alongside a solar system for electric power. It would be quicker, and they could start realizing their dream together sooner. They would also contact a cell company about building a cell tower. That would be a must.

Tyler helped her out of the SUV and pulled her in tight, kissing her soundly. He threaded his fingers through her hair, and their lips danced in tandem, instinctively knowing what to do. She lifted one hand to fan her face, her blush spreading. He smiled, their lips still connected.

"Wanna go hide in the barn?"

Georgia laughed. There was no barn yet. And he was staying true to his word to respect her. But the joke still made her smile.

"Someday we will have a barn, and I'm gonna hold you to that suggestion." Tyler choked a cough, his wide grin telling her he would look forward to that.

A geological survey had found both oil and natural gas under the ranch. Once the wells were in place, the ranch would start producing income almost immediately. The cattle would come later. Georgia was amazed at how God had brought them to this place. Who would have thought just a few short months ago that she would be standing here beside Tyler Boseman Harriman Grant, soon to become his bride? They were truly blessed.

***

THE WEDDING WAS at the Double H, next to the lake where they had their first, and almost last, date. The reception was held in the barn, which was strung with lights and cleaned to make room for dancing. Tents were also set up outside, providing cover from the Texas sun over tables and chairs.

Sam and Ellen embraced Tyler as their new in-law. What had started as a slugfest between Tyler and Sam had become a tight bond. Tyler pitched his new nephew in the air and wondered when he and Georgia would have one just like him.

Tyler's parents and most of his family were there as well. The only one missing was Malcolm, who was in the Army and currently on deployment in an undisclosed location. Tyler had reconciled with everyone and was looking forward to being part of the family again, with Georgia at his side. They had embraced her immediately, and she loved all of her new in-laws.

Amos Carver played for the wedding and the reception with music that kept everyone lively on the dance floor. The cake was three tiers, with four side cakes in various flavors. Mrs. Carson and Mrs. Houston had organized a gift tree. Gifts were stacked on three tables and around them on the floor. It seemed that most of the town had turned out for the celebration.

If you asked anyone attending today, you would think that the whole town had been instrumental in bringing Tyler and Georgia together. The rumor mill was hard at work again, only this time everyone was taking credit for the love story.

Tyler and Georgia thanked everyone for celebrating with them, and swung into their first dance as husband and wife while the band played "Georgia on My Mind." He dropped her into an exaggerated dip and kissed her soundly.

REGGIE WATCHED from the edge of the dance floor as the band broke into "Cotton Eyed Joe." He had stood up beside Tyler as his best man. They had worked together for nearly nine years and he was truly happy for Tyler and Georgia. Normally he would be out there too, boot-scootin' with every single female in attendance, young or old. Today he felt restless. He flipped through several social media posts on his phone when his finger stopped on an advertisement. He usually skimmed right over them, but this one caught his eye.

"OWN YOUR OWN RANCH, NO DOWN PAYMENT. Work alongside current owner for one year, earn 50% interest. Thousand-acre spread. Possible buyout for full ownership after one year. Serious inquiries only. No land sharks."

Interesting. Was this local? He saved the ad in his feed and promised himself to review it again later. Tyler was moving on. Maybe it was time for Reggie to do the same.

## THE END

# ACKNOWLEDGMENTS

It takes a team to produce a book. Sure, the author comes up with an idea, rolls it around in her head for weeks, months, or even years—and finally starts writing. But that's the easy part. Early beta readers will tell you everything that is wrong with the story. Your editor will spellcheck, grammar check, question "Did you really mean to say this?", and then proceed to correct every tiny dot and tittle—or in my case, comma. Any errors in this book are mine, and mine alone.

After editing, your cover designer needs all the data in a specific format, so she can not only design a fabulous cover, but make sure it fits for the genre, marketing strategy, etc. And then all the pieces—the front and back matter, as well as the story itself—has to all be packaged within the cover. Nice and pretty.

I started writing *Rumors of Grace* and the prequel, *A Matter of Trust*, when I retired in 2021. My first draft was rough—really bad, actually. I entered it into a contest and got my first taste of a "thick-skinned" review. But I learned a lot from that feedback.

I applied that feedback when I wrote *House of Cards*. I have other novels in flight—aka *works in progress*—and each one helps me learn more about the craft of creating the kind of story that you want to live in. But my heart went back to the fictional small town of Nora Hills, Texas, and I knew I had to complete this book. I hope you can taste Texas as you read.

To my friends at Safe Harbor Christian Church, thank you

for your constant encouragement. You have often asked for updates, asking "When is your next book coming out?" I'm grateful for your support.

To Kim, my editor, thank you for your extreme patience. I'm still a work in progress, but I'm learning.

To Emilie, my cover designer, you make the prettiest covers. It's an honor to work with you.

To my sweet hubs, thanks for understanding that this is important to me. No, I don't have to write books. I do it because I want to. You understand that. And that means the world to me.

And Jesus, thank for your Grace, and for allowing me to take this amazing ride. Just as you told parables, hopefully you can use my stories to bring the gift of your mercy to those who are searching for you.

# PLAYLIST AND SCRIPTURE

Georgia's Playlist

"(Let's Give Them) Something To Talk About," Bonnie
Raitt, 1991
"Kiss You All Over", Exile, 1978
"I Feel The Earth Move (Under My Feet"), Carole King, 1971
"I Heard It Through The Grapevine," Marvin Gaye, 1968
"I Fall To Pieces," Patsy Cline, 1961
"It's Only Make Believe," Conway Twitty, 1959

The Concert

"Hello, Darlin'," Conway Twitty, 1970
"Desperado," The Eagles, 1973

The Wedding

"Georgia On My Mind," Ray Charles, 1960

Hymns

"In The Garden," Charles Austin Miles, 1912
"Just As I Am,",Charlotte Elliott, 1835

Other Songs

"Twinkle, Twinkle Little Star," Jane Taylor, 1806
"Home On The Range," Dr. Brewster Higley 1871 (lyrics),
Daniel Kelley, 1947 (music)

## THE NORA HILLS TEXAS SERIES

### 2025

*A Matter of Trust* – Rachel and Randall, A Nora Hills Prequel

*Rumors of Grace* – Tyler and Georgia, Book One

*The Gift of Mercy* – Corbett and Denilyn, Book Two, A Christmas Novella

### 2026

*Promise of Honor* – Reggie and Haley, Book Three

*A Place of Peace* – Ritz and Peyton, Book Four

*Whispers of Hope* – Malcolm and Emily, Book Five

*A Thread of Truth* – Caleb and Veeve, Book Six

### ALSO BY RENA BELL YEAGER

*House of Cards* –David and Elizabeth

# THE LOST REPUBLIC

## AN ACE GONZALES NOVEL

# W. J. SPEED

Copyright 2024 W.J. Speed
TLR, LLC.
All rights reserved.

Visit the author at Instagram @thelostrepublic850

The author appreciates the time you've spent reading this story. If you enjoyed it, please consider leaving a review at the place of purchase, and feel free to share it with friends, family, and anyone else who might enjoy it. Recommendations from trusted individuals are among the best ways for readers to find new stories.

Library of Congress Control Number: 9798992031706
Hardback ISBN: 979-8-9920317-2-0
Paperback ISBN:979-8-9920317-0-6
Ebook ISBN: 979-8-9920317-1-3